SAXBY SMART
PRIVATE DETECTIVE

Five
Seconds to
Doomsday

SIMON CHESHIRE

Piccadilly Press • London

First published in Great Britain in 2009
by Piccadilly Press Ltd,
5 Castle Road, London NW1 8PR
www.piccadillypress.co.uk

A catalogue record for this book is available
from the British Library

ISBN: 978 1 84812 027 3 (paperback)

3 5 7 9 10 8 6 4 2

Printed in the UK by CPI Bookmarque, Croydon CR0 4TD
Cover design by Patrick Knowles

INTRODUCTION:
IMPORTANT FACTS

My name is Saxby Smart and I'm a private detective. I go to St Egbert's School, my office is in the garden shed, and this is the sixth book of my case files. Unlike some detectives, I don't have a sidekick, so that part I'm leaving up to you – pay attention, I'll ask questions.

DP

SAXBY SMART
PRIVATE DETECTIVE

The *Saxby Smart – Private Detective*
series:

The Curse of the Ancient Mask
The Fangs of the Dragon
The Pirate's Blood
The Hangman's Lair
The Eye of the Serpent
Five Seconds to Doomsday
The Poisoned Arrow *(October 2009)*

Find fun features, exclusive mysteries
and much more at:

www.saxbysmart.co.uk

Find out more at:
www.simoncheshire.co.uk

Case File Sixteen:

Five Seconds
to Doomsday

CHAPTER
ONE

WHEN YOU'RE A BRILLIANT SCHOOLBOY detective like me, you have to accept the fact that not everyone is going to like you. By that, I don't mean that some people dislike me *personally*. Oh noooo, no, no. I am, of course, enormously popular at school and have loads of friends.

A-hem. A-hem.

What I mean is, a brilliant schoolboy detective like me is bound to make enemies. It's unavoidable. When you go around solving crimes you're going to end up with a whole load of criminals who bear a grudge against you. It goes with the job. It's what I believe is called 'an occupational hazard'.

Most of the time these grudges don't amount to very much: I get a bit of a scowl from one or two of the fellow

5

schoolmates I've successfully brought to justice in the past, but that's normally it. Most of the time, bad guys know they've done wrong and they accept that I'm only doing my job when I unmask them.

However . . .

Now and again I cross swords (as they say) with a villain who's particularly nasty. The sort of pond life who'd try to get their own back on me.

There was the case of the Woodburn twins, Timmy and Jimmy, who'd tried to send their granny mad by pretending there were three of them (it was a trick done with a pair of mirrors and an old curtain, but it's far too complicated to talk about now). After I exposed their little scheme, they started spreading lies about me.

Then there was little baby-faced Michael Gifford, the most innocent-looking kid in the school. He'd hatched an elaborate plan to blackmail an entire class. Once I'd put an end to his plans, he began whacking himself in the eye and telling teachers I'd hit him. Spiteful little so-and-so.

Anyway, none of their evil ideas succeeded.

However . . .

My case file *Five Seconds to Doomsday* reveals all about the worst example of revenge I've ever experienced. This was something altogether different. This was about Revenge, with a capital R. Big time.

It all started on a Friday morning in June, when I was in my Crime HQ – otherwise known as the garden shed – sorting through some notes on a case I'd labelled *The Adventure of the Impossible Hamster*.

Friday morning? What, no school, I hear you cry? No, that particular Friday was what teachers call a 'Teacher Training Day' and what the pupils of St Egbert's call 'Yeehoo, An Extra Day Off For No Reason, Hahaaa, Whoop Whoop'. (Why can't teachers do their training during the school hols? I mean, they get *weeks* off in the summer. *Weeks!* Anyway, whatever the reason, I think it's *great*. More training for teachers, that's what I say!)

For the whole of that Friday, the Head was hosting some sort of meeting/conference/chit-chat involving half the teachers from half the schools in the entire district. Result: freedom for brilliant schoolboy detectives!

So . . . I was trying to concentrate on sorting out my notes, but I kept hearing a noise. A tiny noise, a sort of tapping. It was difficult to make out at first, because it was masked by the noise of the rain outside. The rain had been falling – steadily, heavily, endlessly – since Monday afternoon, and it was really starting to get on my nerves. Wherever you went, you couldn't quite escape the dull drone of battering raindrops.

Tip-tap . . .

There it was again! I looked up from my notes, frowning. Someone at the door? No, in this rain, anyone who arrived at my shed would be banging loudly to be let in.

Was it the creaking of the shed? No, I'd heard that plenty of times and this wasn't the same sound at all.

Tip-tap . . .

It was coming from the corner, by my filing cabinet of case notes.

Tip-tap . . .

Something caught the light. Something small fell from the ceiling.

Tip-tap . . .

I leaped to my feet! That was a drip of water! The roof was leaking!

For a second or two, I hopped about making panicky *ahh-ooo-ulp* noises. The thought of my precious case notes getting soaked and ruined was too awful to bear! *Quick, I thought to myself, find something to catch the drips in.*

Bang, bang, bang! The shed door shook loudly.

'Saxby, you in there?' yelled a voice from outside.

'Come in!' I yelled back. I was hurriedly searching through some of the boxes of DIY and gardening-type stuff, which I'm forced to share with the shed.

In a flurry of rain and a flapping of his big red umbrella, my great friend George 'Muddy' Whitehouse entered and started shaking the rain off his shoes. As readers of my earlier case files will know, Muddy is St Egbert's School's resident expert in all things technical; he's a vital source of useful gadgets when I'm in the middle of an investigation.

'Urgh, it's soaking out there!' he cried.

'It's getting to be the same in here!' I cried. 'A-ha!' I'd found an empty plastic plant pot.

'Never mind that now,' said Muddy, 'I've got an emergency situation!'

'So have I!' I cried. I placed the plant pot underneath the leak. Instead of a *tip-tap*, the drips made a sort of *t-plonk* sound. 'There! What do you think?'

'That's no good,' said Muddy.

'What, you think it's not big enough?' I asked. 'You think the rain will fill it up too quickly?'

'No, it's a plant pot, you twit,' said Muddy. 'It's got drainage holes in the bottom.'

I picked the pot up again. The drips had made a little circular puddle underneath it. Pausing only to let out a yelp of alarm, I went back to searching through the boxes.

'Anyway, are you listening to me?' asked Muddy. 'I said I've got an emergency situation!'

'Yeahyeahyeah,' I said, not looking in his direction for a single moment. 'A-ha!' I'd found a large empty paint

9

tin. I tipped out the load of dust-covered paintbrushes that were inside it and positioned the tin on top of my filing cabinet.

Now the drips went *k-ping*.

'This is terrible,' I muttered, staring at the wet patch on the roof. 'This is a disaster. What am I going to do?'

'Oh, for goodness' sake, it's just a little leak,' scoffed Muddy. 'You can fix that in five minutes.'

For the first time since he'd arrived, I looked directly at Muddy. His eyes were red-rimmed and he was looking almost tearful.

I suddenly felt very guilty. 'I-I'm sorry, Muddy,' I stammered. 'What on earth's the matter? Here, sit on my Thinking Chair.'

He plonked himself down on my battered old leather armchair. I don't think I'd ever seen my friend looking so miserable. My insides stung with nerves as I wondered what could have happened.

'Norman has been kidnapped!' cried Muddy, unable to contain himself any longer.

'Kidnapped?' I gasped in shock. 'Good grief! Why would anyone want to . . . Hang on, who's Norman?'

10

CHAPTER
TWO

FOR A MOMENT OR TWO, Muddy wiped his nose with the back of his hand. The paint tin on the filing cabinet went *k-ping*.

'Do you promise not to laugh?' mumbled Muddy. 'I know what you're like. You'll laugh.'

'I won't, honest,' I told him. 'Who's Norman?'

'My teddy bear,' said Muddy.

'Haaa ha ha ha haaaaaaaa!' I stopped myself. 'Sorry.'

'I've had him since I was a baby!' cried Muddy crossly. 'He's very precious!'

'Yes, I'm sorry,' I said. 'I'm really sorry. I'm being insensitive. Who kidnapped him? And why?'

'I've no idea,' said Muddy. 'That's why I've come straight to you. They've left this note.'

He took a slightly crumpled envelope from the pocket of his raincoat and handed it over. Tucked inside was a piece of paper and a photo, showing a grubby-looking old teddy bear which had lost an eye. And an ear. And some of its fur.

'He's . . . adorable,' I said, with a grim expression on my face.

'No, he's not,' muttered Muddy. 'He smells. But he's my teddy and I want him back.'

I looked more closely at the photo. There were long fingers clutched around the poor bear's neck. In the background was something shiny but a bit out of focus. I set the photo aside and read what had been printed on the sheet of paper:

Whitehouse,

As you can see, I have Teddy. I thought we could play a little game. Let's call it Hunt Teddy.

Here are the rules. At this moment, Teddy is wedged into a specially adapted food blender. It's very similar to the *Whitehouse Whisk-A-Matic* that *you* designed (Oh! How ironic!). Only, this one's got sharp blades instead of plastic paddles. And no stupid sticky letters on the side saying *Whitehouse Whisk-A-Matic*.

Teddy's blender is inside a box, which is hidden at a secret location. At precisely 4 p.m. today, Friday, the timer inside the box will switch the blender on. Teddy will be s-h-r-e-d-d-e-d. Cut to pieces. Unless, that is, you're clever enough to solve the clues correctly and get to him first. Opening the box will disarm the timer and Teddy will be safe. And that's how you play Hunt Teddy! Good game, eh?

Tick tock, time is ticking away. Here's your first question. Ready?

'There's a lady eating chocolate by a blue fence while she waits to travel to London. Where is she pointing?'

Oh, I nearly forgot. There is one more rule. If you tell anyone about the game, anyone at all, then the timer will be adjusted. You'll find out how. If you break the rule, that is. Bye for now.

'What kind of spiteful creature would do this?' I said quietly, frowning to myself. 'So, Muddy, you read this last bit and came straight over here to tell me?'

'Absolutely,' said Muddy. 'I'm not going to let some bullying, kidnapping gutter-slime scare me into doing what he wants! I know it means a risk to poor Norman but, well, this can't be allowed to happen!'

'Quite right.' I nodded. 'Who knows about Norman? Obviously, you don't show him to many people or I'd have seen him before now.'

Muddy shrugged, slightly embarrassed. 'Well, a few.

Now and again. Here and there. Over the years. Norman's very shy, really. He lives under my pillow. When he meets someone, he likes to be properly introduced, by name, and he tells them, in a quiet voice, all about his adventures in —'

'Er, yeah, that's more info than I need, thanks,' I said quickly, holding up both hands to cut him short. 'And what about this *Whitehouse Whisk-A-Matic*? What's that?'

'Oh, just something I knocked together a couple of months ago,' said Muddy. 'It didn't really work. It was supposed to be a sort of automatic tea stirrer but it ended up breaking the cups. It's just stayed in a box in my laboratory.'

I turned the kidnapper's note, and the photo, over and over in my hands. Both had clearly been produced with an ordinary, everyday computer. I couldn't get any clues from the printing or the paper.

However, there were a couple of minor points I could pick up from the note, bearing in mind what Muddy had just told me.

Compare the note to how Muddy answered my last two questions. Do your observations match mine?

'This kidnapper is someone who's been to your house fairly recently,' I said, 'but is not someone you've ever introduced Norman to. That should help us narrow the field of suspects.'

'How do you know that?' said Muddy.

I kept on examining the note in minute detail. Reflections rippled across it from the rain sliding down the shed window. Behind me, drops of water continued to *k-ping* into the empty paint tin.

'The kidnapper obviously doesn't know Norman's name,' I said. 'He just calls him *Teddy*, with a capital T. If he was someone you'd shown Norman to, he'd put *I have Norman*, not *I have Teddy*. And it must be someone who's been in your garage – sorry, your Development Laboratory – within the last couple of months. Otherwise he wouldn't know about the *Whisk-A-Matic*, would he?'

Muddy scratched his head. 'Even so, that doesn't narrow it down all that much. Lots of people visit my lab. I'm always mending things. Am I going to have to do a list of everyone I've done a job for?'

I held the photo up to the light. 'No,' I said quietly, almost to myself. 'I've got a pretty good idea who's behind this already.'

'You have?' asked Muddy.

'Mmm,' I said. 'Notice how this isn't a ransom note.

15

He hasn't kidnapped Norman to get money or anything out of you. So, he's got some other motive. I think it's revenge.'

'Revenge?' gasped Muddy. 'What have I ever done to anyone?'

'I think,' I said, wincing a bit, 'it's because you've helped me a lot in the past. In my investigations. I think the kidnapper knew perfectly well that you'd come straight to me with this. I think he wants revenge on both of us.'

'Who does?' said Muddy.

'That low-down rat Harry Lovecraft,' I said, almost in a whisper. (Readers of my earlier case files will already know about that low-down rat Harry Lovecraft. He was the sneakiest worm in our school, a smarmy no-gooder whose underhand schemes I'd had to put an end to on many occasions.)

At that point, Muddy said several things I can't repeat here. Then he said, 'Of course! I thought there was something odd about the way he just put *Whitehouse* like that. He always calls you "Smart", doesn't he?'

'Exactly,' I said. 'And you see that out-of-focus, shiny thing in the background of the photo? I think that's one of his trademark shiny shoes. I'm guessing this picture was taken looking down at the floor. Probably on a phone, because it's framed long-side-up, and you do that more often with a phone camera.'

I was pretty sure I was right. However, both Muddy and I were slightly shocked that Norman's kidnapper should turn out to be Harry.

'I'm slightly shocked,' gasped Muddy. 'Harry Lovecraft has been behaving himself perfectly all this term. I heard he'd even stopped conning the younger kids out of their dinner money.'

'Yes.' I sighed. 'I'm sure everyone at school has been thinking he's come to his senses and smartened up his act. Obviously, he's been playing us all for fools. He was positively friendly when our year were doing podcasts for the school website the other day. So when has he been to your laboratory, then?'

'About three weeks ago. When we had to do the project on motion and pulleys and all that stuff.'

'Oh yeah.' I nodded. *Design a Vehicle which Will Move under its Own Power.*'

'That's the one,' said Muddy. 'Harry was one of five people from our class who came over after school one Monday. That sneaky piece of poo must have gone nosing around in my room, found poor Norman, and plotted a kidnap.'

'Could be,' I muttered to myself, taking another close look at the photo. 'Exactly when and how were the note and photo delivered to your house? Did they come in the post?'

'No,' said Muddy. 'As it's Friday, my mum's been at work since quite early, and as it's a teacher training day, I've been in my lab since straight after breakfast. Dad was doing the housework with his iPod up loud. He saw an envelope on the doormat at about eleven o'clock. It could have arrived any time after eight-thirty. It just had *G Whitehouse* printed on it. Dad brought it out to me and went back to his vacuuming. I opened it, read it, cried out in horror, and came straight over here.'

'You didn't see Harry, or anyone else, approach the house?'

'No, I was at the workbench at the back of my lab,' said Muddy. 'Someone could easily go to the front door without me spotting them. I'd run an extra power cable from inside the house out to the lab so the door was ajar. Oh no! I even made it easy for Harry to sneak in and take Norman!'

I handed him the note and the photo. 'You mustn't blame yourself. This is absolutely typical Harry Lovecraft nastiness. Although I'm still not sure *why* he's doing it.'

'I thought you said it was revenge,' said Muddy.

'Well, yes,' I said. 'But I can't help feeling he's gone to a lot of trouble just to play a nasty game. Why make it a game anyway? He risks losing, doesn't he? And that would be pretty feeble revenge.'

'Look, this is Harry Lovecraft we're talking about,' said Muddy. 'He'll be one hundred per cent sure he's going to come out on top. He only plays to win. Right?'

'Hmm.' I nodded slowly. 'Worrying, isn't it? For now, all we can do is play along and hope we can get one step ahead of him somewhere along the line. Remind me of that first question he's set you. I mean, us.'

Muddy read it out. 'There's a lady eating chocolate by a blue fence while she waits to travel to London. Where is she pointing?'

'OK, let's think about it logically,' I said.

'How?' cried Muddy. 'It sounds like gibberish.'

'Harry's not going to give us a question we can't answer, is he? Otherwise, why ask it? And anyway, we know he's not cleverer than I am. Soooo . . .' I wrinkled up my nose in thought.

Muddy muttered to himself. 'Why would eating chocolate make you point at something?'

'The box we're looking for is hidden in a secret location,' I said. 'He's leading us somewhere. So my guess is that this question will take us to a *place*.'

'We won't have to go to London, will we?' said Muddy. 'That's miles away!'

'No, no,' I replied. 'I don't think that's what it means.'

Some definite possibilities occurred to me. I could think of at least a couple of places which might fit this clue – real places where this mysterious woman might be waiting.

Are you thinking what I'm thinking?

'I think this refers to a bus depot or a railway station,' I said. 'Somewhere you'd wait to travel.'

'How about the airport?' suggested Muddy. 'Or even a taxi rank? Or maybe this woman's simply got her own car?'

'If she was using her own car, why would she be waiting?' I said. 'And it sounds unlikely that she'd be taking a taxi, not all the way to London.'

'Then what clue do we have to tell us which type of transport it means?' said Muddy. 'The chocolate?'

'The blue fence!' I cried, hopping to my feet. 'Think about the bus station in town. Does that have a fence around it?'

'Er, no,' said Muddy, pulling a quizzical face and glancing at the shed ceiling.

'And neither does the airport,' I said. 'Or rather, it *does* have a fence, ten metres high and covered in razor wire, but it's not blue. We need to go to the train station! That has those metal railings all along the side by the street, doesn't it?! Painted blue!'

'So who's the lady?' said Muddy.

'We'll find out when we get there!' I cried. I flung the shed door open. The rain pattered heavily against the legs of my trousers, blown in by the cold wind. 'Come on, we haven't a moment to lose!'

I stuffed my notebook into my pocket and fetched my

long, flappy, dark green raincoat and matching wide-brimmed hat from the coat stand in the hall.

'Where did you get that hideous raincoat?' gasped Muddy. 'You look like you're dressed up as a giant gherkin.'

I paused, looking down at it with a hurt expression on my face. 'I got it last year on holiday. English seaside resorts are the best places to buy rainwear. What's wrong with it?'

'It's hideous, that's what's wrong with it,' muttered Muddy. 'And that hat is completely —'

'Yeah, yeah, you're starting to sound like Izzy,' I said grumpily. 'What's the time now?'

Muddy checked his watch. 'Eleven fifty-five exactly.'

'Right!' I declared. 'We have four hours and five minutes to save Norman the teddy bear. The race is on!'

CHAPTER
THREE

WE ARRIVED AT THE RAILWAY station about twenty minutes later. Muddy held his big red umbrella down close to his head. The spokes kept prodding at the broad brim of my rain hat.

We hurried through chunky sliding doors into the station's main waiting area and ticket office. To one side of us were a newspaper stand and a large plastic partition, behind which a ticket seller sat reading one of the newspapers. To the other side were screens showing *Arrivals* and *Departures*, and warnings that luggage left unattended would be eaten by a trained leopard. Or something like that. I wasn't really paying attention – Muddy and I were busy looking for the mysterious lady mentioned in the note.

The station had two platforms, one on this side of the railway tracks and one on the other side. An assortment of people with suitcases and shoulder bags were milling about on each platform, checking their watches and looking annoyed. They stood out of the rain, under the huge canopies which covered the central parts of the platforms.

'There are quite a few ladies here,' whispered Muddy. 'But I can't see any of them eating chocolate.'

'Hmm, I wonder,' I mumbled, looking up and down the platforms. 'The note says that the lady is waiting by the blue fence. Let's go and see.'

Pointy-topped metal railings ran all the way along the back of each platform. They were painted an identical, shiny shade of dark blue and were slightly nobbly-looking because the blue had obviously been painted on top of about thirty other coats of shiny paint.

Every few metres, a tall, flat advertising poster box was fitted to the blue fence. The see-through fronts of the boxes were spattered with rain. The raindrops made the person in the nearest advert, who was washing her hair in a jungle waterfall, look like she was crying endless tears.

'You'd think if she was stuck in a jungle,' said Muddy, 'she'd have more urgent things to worry about than the smell of her hair.'

'A-ha!' I said. 'Look!'

Next to the shampoo advert was a washing powder

advert, and next to that was an advert for a really boring-looking novel with a lake on the cover, and next to *that* was a poster for *Cosmik: The Gooey Chewy Bar*. A famous movie actress was popping a slab of the stuff into her enormous mouth, as if she was posting a letter. She had one hand on the chocolate and the other was pointing to another Cosmik bar floating on the left side of the poster.

'Ta-daa! The lady eating chocolate,' I said. 'I should have realised that the lady in the question wasn't a real person. I can't see Harry recruiting helpers into one of his sinister plots, can you? Especially an adult. *Here* is where the note is leading us!'

'Or over there,' said Muddy. He nodded at the opposite side of the railway tracks. A second copy of the Cosmik poster was on display at Platform 2.

'Oh,' I said.

'Here she's pointing one way,' said Muddy, 'and over there she's pointing the other way. Which is right? In any case, all she's pointing at is more chocolate, the greedy pig. Where does that get us?'

For a moment or two, I was in a panic. Then I remembered what the note had said.

'This is the right poster,' I said. 'The note said the lady is waiting to travel to London. You catch trains to London from *this* platform, Platform 1. And as to where she's pointing, obviously it's the *direction* we're interested in, not the chocolate. Although, y'know, I quite fancy some chocolate, mmmm.'

'But the direction she's pointing in only leads back to the ticket office,' said Muddy.

I walked over to the advert, stepping around the puddles of rain. As I approached it, I could see that there was something small taped to the side of the poster box at exactly the spot the woman was pointing to.

It was a folded-up plastic bag. I pulled it free and opened it up. Inside was another envelope, exactly like the one Harry had delivered to Muddy's house. Printed on it, was *G Whitehouse and friend*.

I got a sinking feeling in my stomach. The rain was getting heavier again. Quickly, Muddy and I retreated to the ticket office. We sat on a metal bench beside the sliding doors and opened the envelope.

As I read the printed note inside, that sinking feeling in my stomach got a lot worse . . .

Whitehouse. Smart.

Well done. You got the answer right. But oh dear, oh dear, Whitehouse – I did warn you not to tell anyone, didn't I? You broke the rule, and so the timer in the box is now set to go off at 3 p.m., not 4 p.m. Tick tock, Teddy's time is running out. Meanwhile, welcome to the game, Smart. Here's what *you're* playing for: also in the box, and also connected to the timer, is a cleverly adapted mobile phone. At 3 p.m., as Teddy goes all to pieces, this phone will send an MP3 audio file to everyone in the school, including the Head and all the teachers. It's my secret recording of you being shockingly rude about the Head and confessing that you've framed suspects in the past, made up evidence, that sort of thing. Your days as a detective will be over. You might even get excluded, who knows?

I'm really enjoying this game. Here's your next question:

'Two schoolkids are drinking Italian tea.

They use the code 6-1-2-4-4-7.

Where are they going next?'

Don't forget, you mustn't tell anyone else about the game, and the timer goes off at 3 p.m. on the dot. Opening the secret box and disarming the timer is the only thing that can save the day. Bye for now.

'Saxby!' gasped Muddy, wide-eyed with horror. 'When have you been shocklingly rude about the Head?'

'I *haven't*, you twit!' I cried. 'He hasn't recorded *me*, he's obviously faked my voice. This situation is getting more serious by the minute.'

'Faked your voice?' said Muddy. 'You mean he's impersonated you? Imitated the way you speak?'

'Harry Lovecraft? I don't think so,' I scoffed. 'He

couldn't manage an accent for the last school play. *His* smarmy tones would be far easier to imitate than mine.'

'Then how?' said Muddy.

'Technical know-how?' I shrugged. 'You do that sort of thing every day. Don't you remember, we used your voice-changing gear in the case of *The Hangman's Lair*?' (See Volume Four of my case files.)

Muddy shook his head. 'Making your voice sound different is fairly easy, but making it sound like someone else's is *very* hard. I've tried to make a phone attachment that'll copy my mum's voice so I can call school and give myself permission to be off sick. But I've never been able to make it work.'

'So how's he done it, then?' I said, extremely worried that a low-down rat like Harry Lovecraft might be even better at making gadgets than Muddy. 'And how did he get all the teachers' phone numbers?'

'Actually,' said Muddy, 'it wouldn't be hard. You'd just need to —'

I scrunched up my face for a moment and waved my hands about a bit. 'We mustn't get distracted,' I said. 'Right now, the most important thing is to answer the next question and get one step closer to this secret box. Let me have another look at this new message. *Two schoolkids are drinking Italian tea. They use the code 6-1-2-4-4-7. Where are they going next?*'

'I didn't know tea came from Italy,' said Muddy.

'It doesn't,' I said. 'Let's assume the two schoolkids are you and me. So, where would we . . .? I wonder if it means Lucrezia's, that coffee shop in the mall?'

'Is Lucrezia an Italian name?' said Muddy.

'I think so,' I said. 'I don't really know. But we know someone who will.'

I phoned my other great friend, Isobel 'Izzy' Moustique, that Supreme Ruler of Information City, St Egbert's School's Number One Brainbox. (No, I hadn't forgotten what Harry had said in the note about telling other people. I was simply choosing not to be bullied into playing by his rules.)

After a brief check, Izzy confirmed that I was right about Lucrezia being Italian.

'I was going to call you in a minute anyway, Izzy,' I said. 'Muddy and I have got a teeny tiny bit of a problem.'

I gave her all the details. Once she'd finished grumbling angrily about that low-down rat Harry Lovecraft, she agreed to meet me and Muddy at the coffee shop.

I snapped my phone shut and turned to Muddy.

'Time?' I asked.

Muddy glanced at his watch. 'Eighteen minutes to one.'

'We now have just over two and a quarter hours,' I said. 'We'd better hurry. Harry could have hidden that box anywhere.'

A Page From My Notebook

(A slightly soggy page, because I'm jotting this down on the way to the shopping mall.)

PROBLEM 1: How has Harry made this MP3 audio file? Has he secretly been a better gadget-builder than Muddy all this time? No, that seems highly unlikely. He would surely have got involved in more high-tech crime before now.

POSSIBLE SOLUTION: He's getting help. Was I wrong to think he wouldn't recruit helpers into one of his sinister plots? It would have to be an adult (because of Problem 1), but WHO? I already know that some members of his family are equally sneaky (see the case of *The Fangs of the Dragon*), but we come back to Problem 1 again. It would have to be someone with a lot of technical expertise.

WAIT! POSSIBLE SOLUTION, SECTION B: Am I looking at this the wrong way? Has he done something else entirely? Has he used some other method to create that file? But if so, WHAT? Hmm, am back to square one here!

PROBLEM 2: I still don't understand – WHY stage this horrible GAME? Why go to all this trouble? If Harry wants revenge, why not just shred Norman? Why not just email that MP3 file? And SURELY he realises this could backfire on him? (If Muddy and I succeed, we'll literally have a boxful of evidence against him! And does he REALLY think I, Saxby Smart, couldn't prove that his audio file is a fake?) Harry's sneaky, but he's not stupid. SOMETHING ELSE is going on here. But what?

POSSIBLE SOLUTION? None at all, yet . . .

One thing's for sure: So far, that low-down rat Harry Lovecraft has anticipated our every move PERFECTLY. Need to WATCH OUT!

CHAPTER
FOUR

LUCREZIA'S CAKE 'N' COFFEE IS a cosy little shop. It's tucked away at the back of the town's shopping mall, sandwiched between Everything for a Quid and a shop which sells clocks and watches.

Most of the dark brown floorspace was taken up by a scattering of dark brown tables and chairs. Old-fashioned scenes of Italian cities stood out against the dark brown wallpaper.

To one side was a counter, decked out with all kinds of hissing, shiny chrome coffee machines and teapots. Between the coffee machines and a tall glass case of cakes and pastries, a woman in a dark brown apron hummed cheerily to herself while she gave the counter a once-over with a wet cloth. There were only a handful of customers, all of them with shopping bags beside their feet and a mind-your-own-business look on their faces.

By now, Muddy and I were both hungry. We bought something sensible and nutritious to eat and sat down at a table near the front of the shop.

I sipped my hot chocolate and sliced at my slab of chocolate cake with a fork.

'It's no wonder you're so out of shape,' said Muddy, 'what with all the sugary rubbish you eat.' He took a huge bite out of his jam doughnut. 'Do you think we're supposed to wait for someone?' he whispered.

'Only Izzy,' I said. I took Harry's second message out of my raincoat pocket and read it through again. 'Like I said before, Harry's not going to ask us questions we can't answer, so something in this shop will give us the key to that code.'

Muddy wedged the rest of his doughnut into his mouth and wiped his fingers on his sleeve. 'Maybe it's something to do with the arrangement of the tables? Maybe you count however many along?'

'Good idea,' I said, 'but all the tables are the same. You wouldn't get any sort of actual answer. This code indicates where we go next so it must give us a place name, or a map reference, or simply a direction. Perhaps it's something to do with the pictures on the walls?'

We took a long stare at the pictures. I think we must have looked a bit strange because the woman behind the counter gave us a nervous grin. She reminded me of a frog. I had another forkful of cake.

The code and the pictures didn't seem to fit together either. However, the code had to relate to something *like* the pictures, something that was fixed and didn't change from day to day – because Harry would have to know that his code could be deciphered by Muddy and me whenever we happened to arrive at the shop. I looked around, frowning. What was there, in this shop, that would give us —

'The menu!' I said. I pointed over Muddy's shoulder and he twisted around. 'The food menu. It's painted on to the wall behind the counter. That wouldn't really change.'

'Yeah, loads of words and numbers,' said Muddy. 'Perfect code-type stuff.'

'I think we can discount the numbers,' I said. 'Look, those prices are chalked up, they're probably changed from time to time. It's the words that matter here. This code, 6-1-2-4-4-7, it must translate into letters. Probably a six-letter word. Probably the name of the next location.'

We took a long stare at the food menu. The woman behind the counter gave us another nervous grin.

The words on the menu looked like this:

> Crusty rolls: tuna/cheese/ham fillings
> Home-made tomato soup (with crusty roll)
> Fresh gateaux: chocolate/lemon/black cherry
> Our daily selection of pastries and doughnuts
> Mega-Cookies: choc chip/almond/triple choc
> Sandwich of the Day (in a crusty roll)
> Lucrezia's Special: crusty roll, cake 'n' coffee
>
> We serve a VAST variety of teas and coffees.
> Just ask us for your favourite,
> we'll DEFINITELY have it! (Probably.)

It took me a couple of minutes to spot the simple key to understanding what 6-1-2-4-4-7 meant. But as soon as I spotted it, I had the answer – and the answer was indeed the name of a location. Can you decipher the code?

'Huh?' said Muddy.

'You use the first letter of each line,' I said. '6-1-2-4-4-7. Sixth line down, first letter is *S*. First line down, first letter is *C*. Second line down, first letter is *H*. Then two of the fourth line down, which is *O*. Then line seven, which is *L*.'

'Oh, you're joking,' groaned Muddy.

'The one and only day we're not allowed to be there and that's where he's sending us,' I said.

'But we can't go to the school,' said Muddy. 'The Head's got that whole conference thing going on. The place will be crawling with teachers from miles around.'

'Perhaps that's the point,' I said, glumly. 'We're bound to be found out. So you and I get into trouble while that low-down rat Harry Lovecraft sits at home giggling. It's all part of his nasty game.'

'Couldn't we just go over to his house and thump him until he gives in?' muttered Muddy grumpily.

'We will not resort to violence,' I said, suddenly turning a bit teachery. 'Besides, it'd never work.'

'No, s'pose not,' sighed Muddy. 'He'd set that shredder off by remote control or something like that.'

I didn't say anything to Muddy but I was getting more worried by the minute. At every step of this game it was becoming steadily clearer that Harry had planned his revenge with enormous care. All those recent weeks of friendliness and good behaviour had obviously been a smokescreen to hide his plotting.

I shuddered slightly. I had a feeling that the worst was yet to come.

At that moment, Izzy came bustling into the coffee shop. As usual during non-school time, she was a riot of bright colours, glittery necklaces and chunky rings. Her auburn hair was stacked up into a thing that looked like the top of a pineapple. In one hand she carried a dripping umbrella and in the other a small bag with home-done swirly patterns on it.

'It's tipping down out there now,' she gasped, out of breath. 'I'm glad to be out of it for a while. Do they still do those mega-cookies here?'

I jumped to my feet. 'Good to see you, Izzy. Come on, we're off!'

'Awww,' moaned Izzy.

'We've got to get to school,' said Muddy.

'Why?' asked Izzy.

'We'll tell you on the way,' I said, heading for the shop door. 'Muddy, what's the time now?'

Muddy looked at his watch. 'One twenty-four.'

'One hour thirty-six minutes left,' I said. 'Let's go.'

At the door, Izzy stopped me with a hand on my arm. She looked me up and down. 'Saxby,' she said quietly, 'where did you get that hideous raincoat? You look like you're dressed up as a giant gherkin.'

'Oh, don't you start,' I grumbled. I gave Muddy a frosty look before he could say 'Told you so'.

We marched out into the noisy shopping mall. I heard the two of them muttering behind me.

'When he wants to know the time, why doesn't he just look at his own watch?' mumbled Muddy.

'He likes being dramatic,' said Izzy. 'Bless.'

CHAPTER
FIVE

HALFWAY TO SCHOOL, WE HAD to take cover for a few minutes in an empty bus shelter. The rain was dropping out of the sky as if the clouds had got fed up with their water lying about doing nothing and were having a complete clear-out.

It was 1.33 p.m. Out of her bag, Izzy pulled a small pink netbook computer with flower stickers on the lid.

'After you called me,' she said, 'I did some digging around. There's good news and bad news.'

'Let's have the good news first,' said Muddy. He had to raise his voice above the roar of the rain.

'The good news is that Muddy was right,' said Izzy. 'Faking Saxby's voice would be extremely difficult. It's not like you see it in movies. You'd need to be a real expert. So, unless Harry has got a real expert working for him . . .'

'I'm not ruling anything out yet,' I mumbled.

'What's the bad news?' said Muddy.

'The bad news is that Harry doesn't need a real expert anyway. I've found out how he could have made that audio file at home using only a computer, some free software and a few hours of spare time.'

'How?' I asked.

'Remember what we were doing at school only the other day?' said Izzy.

I slapped my forehead. That hurt a bit so I rubbed it instead. 'Podcasts!' I groaned. 'For the school website. Arggh, I should have realised!'

'You mean he's edited your podcast?' said Muddy. 'To make it sound like you're saying different things?'

'Yup,' said Izzy.

'He'd need to use software that could balance out any funny-sounding chops and cuts in sentences,' said Muddy, 'but it's do-able. Difficult, but do-able.'

'Are you sure about this?' I said to Izzy. 'Half the class recorded a podcast and none of them included anything even remotely useful for the sort of message Harry's talking about.'

'Oh yeah?' said Izzy. She switched on her netbook. 'I'll download your podcast and send it to your phone.

Listen to it carefully. Meanwhile, I'll see if I can find out anything about this conference of teachers that the Head is hosting at school. It might give us some useful info for when we get there.'

'Good idea,' I said.

I flipped open my phone. As I listened to what I'd recorded for the school website, my heart began to sink. By the time I'd finished, my heart couldn't have sunk any lower without flopping out of the soles of my feet.

Here's a printed version of what I said in the podcast (or a 'transcript', as Izzy says I'm supposed to call it):

Hello! My name is Saxby. Saxby Smart. I'm in Mrs Penzler's class at St Egbert's. I've been a brilliant schoolboy detective for a while now and I've solved loads of crimes. If you've been robbed, or been accused of something awful, or even lost something utterly valuable, I'm the one who you should see. I gather up the evidence and I get to make a . . . Pardon? Oh. Mrs Penzler says I'm supposed to talk about school, not myself. OK. Here goes. This school is pretty good. I mean, some things are stupid, or boring, but mostly it's pretty good . . . What? . . . I know, but shouldn't we be honest with people? . . . Oh . . . Apparently, the Head wants us to mention the very high quality school dinners . . . Really? She's sure about that? . . . Well, OK, today I had a dollop of what might have been pie, but there was a big lump of fat in it, so it was . . . What?

You want me to stop now? . . . Oh . . . Well, so long, folks, this is Saxby Smart saying goodbye.

It would have been very easy indeed for Harry to extract a totally different, rude-about-the-Head or I-framed-a-suspect message from that podcast. In fact, there were loads of possible messages!

How many can you spot?

I didn't have a mirror handy but I'm pretty sure that my face was going very pale. I listened to the podcast again, just to make sure I wasn't making a mistake.

No. No mistake. Amongst the many rearranged phrases that Harry could have extracted from my podcast were such gems as . . .

- Mostly I make up evidence . . .
- I know I'm not supposed to but so what . . .
- The Head is a big fat stupid dollop . . .
- She's awful, so utterly boring . . .
- And Mrs Penzler is very stupid . . .
- The evidence I make up is pretty good . . .
- I've accused some people of crimes but I've not had good evidence so I've had to make things up . . .
- I know I shouldn't talk about it but I'm not honest with people . . .
- If people in this school get to know about me it's goodbye brilliant schoolboy detective . . .

I'm sure there are more – I'll leave it up to you to find them – but that was enough for me.

I slipped my phone back into my pocket. I was feeling slightly dizzy and I don't think it had anything to do with how much chocolate I'd eaten at the coffee shop.

That low-down rat Harry Lovecraft seemed to be not just one step ahead of me but half an Olympic marathon! His revenge was taking shape before my very eyes. Well, my very ears, anyway. How could I possibly . . .

No, wait a minute. I pulled out my notebook and looked at the slightly soggy stuff I'd written down after leaving the railway station.

There was still Problem 2 to consider. And, as far as I could see, this problem had now become worse. If the MP3 file he'd made was almost certainly reconstructed from a school podcast (I thought to myself), it would now surely be *easier* for me to prove that this audio file was a fake. Surely, with the podcast to hand, I was in a *better* position to prove that the MP3 file was all Harry's doing.

A question popped into my head: How does he expect to get away with all this?

Now, more than ever, I was convinced that there was an extra element to Harry's revenge. There had to be something I hadn't yet bargained for, something I still hadn't even guessed at . . .

'I think the rain's easing off a bit,' commented Muddy.

'Right, we'd better go,' I said. I pulled down the brim of my rain hat and turned up the collar of my coat.

The three of us set off at a quick walking pace. Rainwater splashed around our feet.

'Did you find anything about the Head's conference?' I asked Izzy.

'Yes,' she said, hoisting her bag on to her shoulder. 'All the details were on a teachers' bulletin board. St Egbert's is hosting a thing called *Implementing New Technology in the Classroom*. There are about fifty teachers and other Heads attending, along with people from several companies who are demonstrating a load of high-tech computer hardware.'

'Ooooh, that sounds good,' said Muddy, his eyes suddenly sparkling with gadgety glee.

'That sounds unbelievably boring,' I said. 'However, it also sounds like all these teachers will be in one place, not spread all over the school. That might well give us an advantage.'

'They'll be using the main hall,' said Izzy. 'It's the only indoor area big enough.'

None of us spoke again until we reached the school gates. The time was 1.47 p.m.

We hurried over the zebra crossing, which spanned the main road outside the school. The gates were closed, but not locked. As soon as we approached them, we spotted a plastic bag taped to the familiar metal sign which said, *Max Speed 5 mph. No deliveries this entrance.*

Muddy and Izzy held their umbrellas above us as I unfolded the bag. Inside was a third envelope. This one

45

was labelled *G Whitehouse, S Smart and friend*.

I opened the envelope with a feeling of absolute dread. Once again, that low-down rat had correctly anticipated me – he'd known all along that I'd go straight to Izzy for information. The note inside said:

Whitehouse. Smart. Moustique.

Well done. Another correct answer. But, dear, dear me, you've broken the rule *again*.

Welcome to the game, Moustique. The prize you're playing for is this: a second specially adapted phone, also tucked away in the secret box. When the timer goes off, this phone will upload a series of articles to several online encyclopedias. These uploads will be identical to some of your recent school projects. Oh dear, you'll appear to have cheated by copying work from the internet. Tut tut, naughty.

Don't forget, players, that opening the secret box to disarm the timer is the only thing that can prevent me winning the game. I'm feeling generous so I'll tell you that your quest is almost at an end. The box is hidden somewhere in the school. I'll give you a big hint: go to the staff room. Bye for now.

Oh, I nearly forgot. Because you broke the rules again, the timer in the box is now set to go off at 2 p.m., not 3 p.m.

'*What?!*' yelled Izzy.

'That rotten, stinking, low-down rat wants revenge on all three of us!' I cried.

Muddy looked at his watch. 'Look, I hate to say this, guys, but it's now one forty-nine! We have *eleven minutes*!'

Eleven minutes to stop Izzy being made to look like a cheat, to stop me being made to look like an even bigger cheat, and to stop Norman the teddy bear being sliced up into tiny little bits of fluff.

We had to get to the staff room, fast. And without being spotted.

CHAPTER
SIX

TEN MINUTES, FIFTY-TWO SECONDS . . .

We raced across the car park at the front of the main
school building. Luckily, with the Head's conference in full
swing inside, the car park was full to bursting point. If we
kept low down as we ran, no passing teacher would be
able to spot us. Unluckily, keeping ourselves bent double
like that sent the rain trickling icily around our necks.

We crouched behind a rusty yellow Audi. 'The big
danger point is right over there,' I whispered. 'The
windows in the short corridor bit which joins this
building to that one. That corridor bit is right beside the
office and the main hall, and from inside you can see the
car park, the school gates *and* the back entrance that
leads on to the park. There's no escape for us if someone

happens to walk through there. We'd be seen instantly and thrown off the school grounds.'

The staff room was tucked away in the building to our right, at the far end of a long row of classrooms. We would have to run, in plain sight of those windows, for about fifty metres before we could duck out of sight again.

'I can't see anyone, can you?' whispered Izzy.

'Ready?' said Muddy.

'Go!' I cried.

The three of us hurtled over the open patch of ground. I tried to concentrate on where I was going. I dared not glance over my shoulder at the windowed corridor. My nerves sizzled. I was terrified I'd hear a muffled 'Oi!' behind me at any second.

Gasping for breath and soaking wet, we scuttled into the building under a covered walkway and took shelter in the art room. We hid behind the cupboards where all the painting stuff was kept.

It felt weird being in the school when there were no other students around – the same way it feels weird if you've got an appointment in school time and you suddenly realise that everyone else is in lessons. The only sounds were the dripping of raindrops off our noses and the creaking of my raincoat as I shifted my weight.

'Eerie, isn't it?' whispered Muddy. His voice echoed

off the whitewashed brick walls.

I looked at my watch. Nine minutes, four seconds . . .

We crept out of the art room, our heads flicking in different directions to watch out for signs of teachers. To one side of us was the long row of empty classrooms, which we'd need to pass.

Opposite us was the door to the girls' toilets. It had been wedged open and from one of the cubicles came a steady series of clanks, bumps and swearwords. Apparently the school caretaker was using the day to catch up on some maintenance work on the plumbing. He seemed to be having trouble with something called a wretched blasted compression joint.

I put a finger to my lips to tell the others to stay quiet. I pointed towards the classrooms and we tiptoed past the open toilet door. The caretaker's attention was elsewhere but any noise would have quickly brought him out to investigate.

Our tiptoeing got steadily faster as we advanced. The door to the staff room was also open but as we got closer we could see that the place was empty.

Seven minutes, twenty-one seconds . . .

We edged into the room, still keeping a sharp eye out in all directions. I'd only been in here a couple of times before. There was a kitchen area to one side and lines of low, airport-style seats almost everywhere else. Coffee tables punctuated the rows like full stops in a paragraph.

'Anyone see the next message?' whispered Izzy.

'I think this must be it,' I said, walking over to one of the coffee tables. Sticky-taped among the brown mug-rings was a sheet of A4. All that was printed on it was . . .

Text me.

. . . followed by a phone number. We glanced nervously at each other. Was this some new trick? Why the sudden change of tactics?

'Right,' said Muddy, switching his phone on. 'I'm going to send him the rudest text in history!'

'Wait!' cried Izzy. 'What if it's a trap? What if calling that number sets off the timer in the box?'

Muddy stopped pressing buttons and stood still. 'Could be. That would be typical Harry Lovecraft, that would! Getting us to spring his own trap is exactly the sort of thing he'd do.'

'Or is that what he wants us to think?' I muttered. 'You're right, that number could be a trap. But if we stand around here debating, that timer is going to go off anyway. I think maybe he's just trying to make us waste time. I think we have to risk it.'

Muddy handed me the phone. 'You can risk it, then. I'm not going to.'

With my heart thumping like a speeded-up hammer, I tapped out *We're here*, entered the number, and . . . My thumb hovered shakily for a moment, then pressed *Send*.

For several seconds, there was absolute silence.

The three of us stared at each other, scared at what might happen next, hardly taking a breath.

Five minutes, forty-one seconds . . .

The silence seemed to squeeze us, like the coils of a snake. I half-closed my eyes. *I've got it wrong*, I thought, my stomach twisting into a knot, *I've got it badly wrong*.

BEEEEP!

All three of us yelped with fright. I almost dropped the phone. *1 Message* flashed on its screen. I didn't recognise the mobile number.

Nice text, Smart. So full of news. Here's the final round, you giant gherkin. The box is under the Head's conference table. Hurry up, not long now. Bye.

Izzy went pale. I think she nearly went 'Wuaaahh' too, but she stopped herself in time. 'The box is in the middle of the Head's conference of teachers?' she cried. 'There's no way we can get to it there!'

'We'll just have to gatecrash,' said Muddy sternly.

'This is another Harry Lovecraft trick, isn't it?' cried Izzy. 'We can't disarm the timer without gatecrashing the conference. And if we gatecrash the conference, we'll be in all kinds of trouble! *That's* why he's been playing this game with us! He's made sure he can't lose, either way!'

I was only half-listening to what Izzy was saying.

Something had just struck me about the text message from Harry. Something very, very important.

My eyes almost popped out and rolled across the carpet. A simple deduction based on two things in the text sent me spinning around, looking wildly in all directions.

Have you worked it out too?

'What are you doing?' asked Izzy.

'He's right here,' I gasped. 'Harry's here in the school too – he can *see* us.'

'Can't see *him*,' said Muddy, peering out of the staff room window. 'Why do you say that?'

'He called me a giant gherkin, just like you two did,' I said. 'So he's seen me. And he knew it was *me* who'd texted, even though I used Muddy's phone. I tell you, he's *watching* us! I bet he's been hiding around here all along!'

'Wherever he is,' cried Izzy, 'we've got four and a half minutes before the timer goes off!'

I took one last lightning look around. Where was Harry watching us from? He was probably some distance away because he wouldn't want to get too close and risk us catching him. From the staff room window, I could see a multitude of places where someone might be able to observe us. Wait! Was that low-down rat in one of the classrooms on the other side of the playground? Was that a glint of light I could see, like a reflection, perhaps off —

'*Come on!*' cried Izzy, dragging at my arm.

The three of us ran out of the staff room and back the way we had come. We skidded to a halt (as quietly as it's possible to skid to a halt) when we saw that the caretaker was now laying out a load of plumbing tools and copper pipes in the corridor outside the girls' toilets, his back towards us. It was sheer chance that he hadn't already seen us, but our route to the main hall was now blocked.

Panic froze my brain for a moment, but then I bounded over to the nearest window. 'Out this way,' I said. 'We'll have to circle the building from outside.'

One by one, we tumbled out on to the tarmac. The rain fell in a curtain of droplets from a broken section of guttering up above us. Water giggled and gurgled along the covered drains beneath our feet.

We splashed our way around the perimeter of the building, keeping below window level as much as we could. For some peculiar reason, I kept thinking about the maths lessons we'd done on calculating circumferences and areas. I suppose I was trying to work out how much more time this longer route would take us, but my brain wouldn't co-operate.

'This longer route will take us at least two minutes more,' said Izzy, above the noise of the rain. 'Anyone come up with an idea yet for gatecrashing that conference without giving the Head a screaming fit?'

'Nope,' said Muddy and I together.

'Me neither,' muttered Izzy sadly.

Two minutes, nineteen seconds . . .

We got back into the building through the door marked *Exit Only*. We were right beside the short building-to-building corridor, the one we'd had to avoid being seen from when we were back in the car park.

Our footsteps echoed off the corridor's sides. I suddenly stopped.

'Izzy,' I cried. 'Stay right here! Don't move off this spot!'

'What? Why?' she asked.

'Remember, you can see both gates from here,' I said. 'Watch for Harry! Don't let him get away!'

'For crying out loud, Saxby,' grumbled Izzy, 'haven't we got more important things to think about? We're at two minutes exactly!'

'Please! Just stay there!' I told her.

Muddy and I dashed ahead. The distance from the corridor, past the school office, to the big double doors of the main hall, was only about ten or fifteen metres.

A low murmur of voices came from inside the hall. Muddy and I crouched beneath the large glass panels that were set into both the doors and the walls to each side. We glanced back. From here, we could still see Izzy. She egged us on with a silent flapping of hands.

The glass panels had posters and notices sticky-taped all over them. I edged myself up until I could see into the hall through a slim vertical gap between a couple of handwritten announcements.

One minute, forty-one seconds . . .

The hall was packed with people. I could see several St

Egbert's teachers, including Mrs Penzler. Every one of them was sitting at a separate small desk, with a laptop in front of them. At the front of the hall was a long series of tables, covered in spotless white tablecloths. On them were an array of screens, keyboards and other computer equipment. A man in a dark suit was standing up and addressing the audience, a huge diagram of a computer network projected up behind him. The Head was sitting behind the table next to him. Out of sight, under that table, had to be the hidden box.

'How are we going to do this, then?' whispered Muddy. 'Just go right in? Try to attract someone's attention?'

Now that I'd seen what was going on in the hall, my mind started firing questions at me about everything that had happened so far. *Why* had Harry set up such a strange and complex revenge? *Why* lead us *here* today, to the Head's conference? *Was* there a hidden motive behind this game?

'Well?' whispered Muddy.

One minute twenty-eight seconds . . .

My head was so full of questions I couldn't think straight. One thought kept nagging away at me: that we *could* win this game, that it *was* still possible to have this whole situation backfire in Harry's face.

And that just didn't fit! So *what* was I missing?

Suddenly, it hit me.

57

I realised I might have been looking at this problem from the wrong point of view.

What if the *box* was the trap? What if opening the box was what Harry *wanted* us to do?

'Muddy,' I said. 'Tell me again. What did you do after your dad gave you that first note this morning?'

'You what?' spluttered Muddy.

'Tell me!'

One minute, nineteen seconds . . .

'I opened the envelope, I read the note, I came straight to your shed! You *know* that!'

'You didn't look for Norman?' I asked. 'You didn't search the house?'

'Why would I? I had that photo right in front of me! I came straight to your shed! Come *on*, we've got to get into the hall!'

I looked straight at Muddy. 'Phone your dad.'

'Are you taking the mickey?' gasped Muddy angrily.

'Do it! We have just over a minute! If I'm wrong, we can still get in there and disarm that timer. Call him!'

Muddy's face was a shifting storm of anger and confusion. He pressed a couple of buttons on his phone. A couple of seconds later he was saying, 'Dad? It's me.'

'Tell him to look under your pillow!' I hissed. 'Quick!'

Muddy stared doubtfully at me. 'Dad, can you go and look under my pillow? Don't ask why, please just do it as

58

fast as you can . . . What? . . . Oh . . .' Muddy turned to me. 'He says he's in the car. He's been to SuperSave. He's just parked outside our house.'

'Well, tell him to *hurry*!' I gasped.

Muddy went back to the phone. 'Dad, can you hurry? I need you to look under my pillow . . . Yes, I know you've got stuff that needs to go in the fridge, but this is urgent . . . Yes, right now . . .'

Seconds ticked by.

Twenty-four seconds.

Twenty-three seconds.

I peeked into the hall again. The man in the dark suit was still talking.

'Dad? . . . No, you can't ring me back . . . I'm at school . . . Yeees, I know, it's a long story, I'll tell you later, but right now —'

Izzy's voice, half whisper and half shout, came from the corridor. 'What are you doing? Get in there!'

I signalled for her to hang on.

'Saxby, for Pete's sake, get to that timer!' she squeaked. 'We'll just have to get into trouble and face the consequences. We can't let that thing go off!'

I didn't know what to do. Should I rush into the hall anyway? What if I was wrong again?

I needed an answer from Muddy's dad!

Fourteen seconds.

'No, Dad,' said Muddy into his phone, 'leave the milk for a minute, go upstairs . . . Yes, it's important, I promise you . . .'

An icy layer of sweat seemed to have suddenly formed all over me. I judged that five seconds would be just enough. It would take five seconds to burst into the hall, dive under the table and fling open the box. The five-second point was my final deadline. Five seconds to doomsday.

My eyes were glued to my watch.

Nine seconds.

Eight seconds.

I had to make a decision. Now. Was I right? Had I now spotted the truth? Was the box a trap? But if so, how? Or had everything Harry said been true?

Seven seconds.

I made my decision.

What do you think is the right thing to do?

CHAPTER
SEVEN

FOUR SECONDS.

The deadline had passed. It was now too late to stop the timer. *If* Harry had told the truth. *If* I was wrong.

Polite applause started up in the hall. I peeped up through the glass panel again. The man in the dark suit had sat down. The Head was on her feet.

Two seconds.

One second.

Two o'clock.

I stared at the white cloth covering the Head's table. I strained to hear any sound which might be coming from underneath it. The teachers' clapping subsided as the Head held up a hand.

No muffled sound of a teddy shredder. No teachers'

phones going off.

'Well, it's two now,' said the Head. 'We'll have a fifteen-minute break, and then we'll be hearing about trends in classroom software.' Dozens of chairs scraped against the hall floor.

Muddy was still on the phone. 'Dad? . . . At last! Well? . . . What? . . . Are you sure? . . . No, no, that's fine. I'll see you later.'

He switched the phone off and turned to me with a look of utter astonishment on his face. 'Norman's there. Under my pillow. As usual.'

I almost collapsed on the floor with relief. I suddenly realised I hadn't taken a breath for about half a minute. My legs started feeling shaky. 'I was right,' I said at last. 'I knew it. Everything Harry told us was a lie. This was all one gigantic con.'

'But . . .' began Muddy. He stopped, confused. 'But . . .' he began again.

'What's going on?' called Izzy from the corridor.

'Keep a look-out!' I called back. 'Harry could make a run for it! Don't lose him!'

'But . . .' said Muddy. 'How did he get Norman back into my room?'

'He never *took* Norman,' I said. 'He never copied your *Whisk-A-Matic*, he never altered my podcast, none of it.'

'So, there's no box under that table?' asked Muddy.

'Oh, there's a box all right,' I said confidently. 'I just don't know what's in it.'

At that moment, the double doors to the assembly hall swung open and the severe shape of Mrs Penzler was looming over us. 'Saxby! George!' she barked. 'Is that Isobel over there? What's going on? You three are in very hot water!'

'Could we have a quiet word, Mrs Penzler?' I said, beaming her my very best lost-puppy-dog smile.

A few quiet words later, Mrs Penzler was having trouble believing me. I couldn't say I blamed her. 'I know you and Harry Lovecraft aren't exactly best friends, Saxby,' she said, 'but you can't seriously be accusing him of something so . . . peculiar. Not without proof.'

'What about the three printed notes?' said Muddy.

'That's not proof, George,' said Mrs Penzler. 'Anyone could have composed those. The same goes for the text you received. If you could show me that the phone which sent the text was Harry's, that would be different. But you can't, can you? The caller's ID is simply a mobile number. I still can't believe anyone would go to so much trouble.'

'Ah, but that's the point, Mrs Penzler,' I said. 'The only definite trouble he's gone to is that box that's still under the table.'

'Can I stop watching the gates now?' called Izzy from the corridor.

'No!' I cried. 'He'll make a run for it as soon as he realises his plan's gone wrong. That could be any second.'

I marched into the assembly hall. Most of the teachers, including the Head, had gone off to find coffee and grumble about the government. I went over to the table at which the Head had been sitting and took hold of the lower edge of its long, white tablecloth.

'You do realise, Saxby,' said Mrs Penzler in a low voice, 'that if we look under here and there's no box, I'll have to conclude that you've fabricated this whole story to cover up whatever the real reason is for your unauthorised presence in school today.'

I smiled weakly at her. With a flourish, and a heart-tearing hope that I wasn't wrong, I lifted the tablecloth.

Muddy, Mrs Penzler and I bent down to look under the table. An opaque plastic storage box, about forty centimetres wide and about twenty centimetres deep, was taped to the underside of the table with thick black tape.

'Do you have any scissors, Mrs Penzler?' I said quietly.

Blinking with alarm at our discovery, Mrs Penzler scurried to the nearby office. I soon had the box cut free and on the floor of the hall. Its lid was fastened shut with a large flip-up catch.

Mrs Penzler reached out towards it.

'*Nooo!*' I cried. A couple of visiting teachers started giving us funny looks. Mrs Penzler snatched her hand back as if the box was red hot. 'Don't open it here, whatever you do! That's what Harry wanted!'

I picked up the box carefully. It was quite heavy, but I couldn't feel anything shifting around inside or hear anything rattle.

I carried it out of the hall, past the office, past a startled-looking Izzy ('Stay there!' I reminded her. 'Keep looking!'), and out into the open air. The rain had eased off a little. I put the box down in the middle of a grassy patch. Mrs Penzler handed me a long twig that had been blown from one of the nearby trees.

Crouching down, I held the twig at arm's length and hooked one end of it under the plastic catch. I paused for a moment. I suddenly remembered I had no idea exactly what was going to be inside this box.

I flipped the catch up.

Instantly, the lid sprung back like a jack-in-the-box. A spray of firework sparks jetted upwards, but were quickly engulfed by a thick, choking column of black smoke, which erupted into the air like a miniature volcano. The smoke snaked its way in a curling cloud up to roof height.

'What the . . .' gulped Mrs Penzler. I'd never seen her with her jaw dangling loose before. Not a pretty sight.

'Wow,' said Muddy. 'A smoke bomb. Well, a smoke grenade, technically.'

'Where did he get a smoke grenade?' I said, astonished,

watching the black cloud slowly dissipate and dissolve into the rain.

'Oh, you can make them,' said Muddy cheerily. 'Yeah, some sugar, baking soda, powdered dye, a few other odds and ends. Not difficult.' The box had stopped gushing now and Muddy peered at what was inside. 'Mind you, most of this has been bought. Look, those fireworks were hooked up to the spring that blew the lid. Simple, but effective. No timer needed, just open the box and whoosh. No wonder that low-down rat was paying close attention when he came to my laboratory. I don't understand *why* he made this thing, though.'

Suddenly, Izzy's voice yelled from the corridor. 'There he is! Heading for the back gate!'

'Right!' grunted Muddy, leaping to his feet.

Harry must have seen the smoke and realised his scheme had been foiled. I followed Muddy as fast as I could, back into the corridor and out the other side of the building.

Muddy was much faster on his feet than me. By the time I was outside again, he was already racing along the path which led away from the building.

A shadowy figure was rapidly crossing the lawn beside the school's back gate. With a flying leap, Muddy knocked the figure flat like a bowling ball cannoning into the pins. I heard a scream of anger, followed by a long, howling 'Eeeuurgghh!'

The reason for the 'Eeeuurgghh!' became clear as soon as Muddy returned. Sure enough, he was hauling Harry Lovecraft along with him, one hand gripping tightly on to the back of that low-down rat's collar.

Both of them were – eeeuurgghh – smeared from head to foot in thick, greenish mud. Muddy's flying tackle had sent the pair of them sprawling across the soaking wet lawn. As readers of my earlier case files will know, no amount of dirt or grime ever worried Muddy. Harry Lovecraft, on the other hand, had other ideas.

'These clothes are ruined!' he spat. 'You two are paying to replace them!'

His expression was as sneering as ever and his voice as slimy as a bucket of greased slugs. The look of disdain in his eyes could still have made a vampire shudder, but the normal gleam of his black hair was streaked with bits of lawn. He was wearing his trademark shiny shoes, and a stripy tie, both splattered in mud. A pair of binoculars hung around his neck.

'So nice to see you again, Harry,' I said with a smile.

'Drop dead,' he sneered, as Izzy and Mrs Penzler hurried over to us. Muddy quickly whispered in my ear.

The conference of teachers was returning to the main hall now, chatting in little groups, ready to hear more about the latest exciting developments in the world of education. Yawn. Mrs Penzler led us to the nearest classroom, stopping off briefly at the loo to gather paper towels for mud-scraping duty.

'The first thing I want,' said Mrs Penzler, putting on her I'm-A-Teacher-Don't-Mess-With-Me-Buster voice, 'is an explanation from you, Harry Lovecraft, as to why you're here at school today.'

Harry perched uncomfortably on a paper towel. He shrugged. 'I forgot it was a teacher training day. Sorry about that.'

'And it took you five hours to work that out?' asked Mrs Penzler sarcastically. 'Did you have anything to do with the box that Saxby and I found in the assembly hall?'

'I don't know anything about any box,' smarmed Harry.

'Then why were you running away?' asked Mrs Penzler.

'I was hurrying home, out of the rain.'

Mrs Penzler snorted. She was getting frustrated.

'Why?' she barked. 'Why would anyone do such an utterly dangerous, irresponsible, stupid, malicious —'

'I think I've worked that one out now,' I piped up. 'We know that Harry wanted —'

'*Someone* wanted,' sneered Harry.

'OK,' I said. '*Someone* wanted revenge on me. And revenge on my friends, too, who've helped me in my past investigations. But what form of revenge would be suitable? Something that would finish me as a detective, that's for sure. And something that couldn't be traced back to this *someone*, either.

'It was the way the rain dissolved that smoke which gave me the final clue. I couldn't work out *why* Harry – sorry, *someone* – had led us here, to school, today of all days. But imagine the scene: big conference of teachers, lots of important people, the Head, and all of them sitting there surrounded by an absolute tonne of high-tech gear. Suddenly, in bursts Saxby Smart! Don't panic, everyone, he cries! All under control! Then he dives under the table, pulls down the box and – thinking he's disarming a timer – he opens the lid. Whoosh! Smoke everywhere. What happens next?'

'The fire alarm goes off!' answered Muddy.

'Exactly,' I said. 'And then . . .?'

Izzy gasped. 'The sprinklers come on, thinking there's a fire.'

'Exactly,' I said. 'And then . . .?'

'That section of the school gets sprayed with thousands of litres of water,' said Izzy.

'Exactly,' I said. 'Every last bit of computer equipment in that hall gets ruined. It might as well have been left out in the car park under the rain. There's thousands of pounds – maybe hundreds of thousands of pounds – of damage. Not to mention the damage to the building!

'And it would all be Saxby Smart's fault. I could explain

all I liked, but I'd have no proof that this *someone* had put me up to it. And anyway, would anyone listen when there was an eye-wateringly huge bill to pay and a school to repair? Plus, I'd have to admit to the world that I'd been totally fooled. My days as a detective would be pretty much over. I might well get booted out of St Egbert's.'

'But why would *someone* make up an elaborate game in order to pull such a stunt?' asked Muddy. 'Couldn't they just, I dunno, say a pet bunny was trapped in the box and needed rescuing?'

'No,' I said, 'because this *someone* knows me too well. I'd start asking questions, wouldn't I? I'd start investigating. No, this *someone* had to wind me up – and you and Izzy, too – so that we'd be in a right panic. He had to get us believing that time was running out, and that if the box wasn't opened right there and then in the assembly hall, bad things would happen.

'Sure, yeah, he *could* have kidnapped Norman, and he *could* have altered my podcast, and he *could* have made Izzy look like a cheat. He *could* have threatened all sorts of things. The point is we had to *believe* it. He had to make us believe that we, personally, were going to suffer if that box didn't get opened in time.

'Of course, all that stuff about teddy bears and podcasts would be small-time stuff next to the smoke trick, right? But only he would know that. All along, I've been wondering to myself why he'd set up such a complex game when he seemed to have relatively little to gain from it. Until I realised the truth: that the entire thing, start to finish, was a con. A series of tricks to stop us thinking straight, so we'd walk blindly into the trap.

'He must have been planning it for ages, waiting for good ideas to pop up. As you suspected, Muddy, he must have gone nosing around when he visited your lab. He found Norman, saw the kidnap-plot potential, and took a picture there and then, just on the off-chance. Same thing the other day, when our class did those podcasts. He saw that re-editing my recording was possible. He knew that he could upload entries to online encyclopedias. He didn't have to actually *do* any of these things, just make sure that they were things we'd believe.

'He waited until he had enough good ideas to piece together his game. He acted friendly with everyone for weeks so that when the game was sprung on us, we'd believe it. He knew we'd believe he'd double-cross us, and that we'd think to ourselves, "Hah! That low-down rat's been pretending all along, and now he's kidnapped Norman," and so on, and so on.'

'Can I go now?' sneered Harry. 'I'm wet and muddy, and having to listen to one of Smart's dribbling speeches is only making matters worse. You have absolutely no proof to link me to this barmy scheme and you know it.'

Mrs Penzler sighed. 'I'm afraid Harry is right,' she said, reluctantly. 'Saxby, it's all very well you and your friends making these claims, but it's well-known that the three of you have plenty of reasons to dislike Harry. Unless you can produce solid evidence, we're going to have rather a long talk, you and I.'

I looked at Muddy. Muddy looked at me. He tried not to giggle. Remember how he whispered to me after he'd caught Harry . . .?

'Come on, then, Smart,' smirked Harry. 'Produce evidence.' He stood up, arms wide, and twirled on the spot. 'Look at me, the only thing I've got are my binoculars. I've been bird watching.'

'In the rain?' I said. 'You've been lying low in an empty classroom, waiting for us to turn up in the staff room. You left a note to text you, so you'd know we'd arrived and that it was time for you to come out of hiding and watch your revenge cause chaos in the assembly hall.'

'I see,' grinned Harry. 'So, where's my phone? Have I swallowed it? Is it concealed inside a hollowed-out tooth?' He took off his coat and handed it to Mrs Penzler, turned out his pockets, rolled up his sleeves and his trousers and rolled down his socks.

'I'm getting fed up of the way you pick on me, Smart,' he slimed. 'Happy now? Have you humiliated me enough?'

Before he could wriggle out of the way, I took hold of

his tie. The look on his face changed from anger to horror. He tried to snatch it away from me, but I flipped it over and slipped a small phone from a slim pocket that had been sewn on its reverse side.

'Muddy felt it when he hauled you over here,' I said. 'Great hiding place. That's what I almost admire about you, Harry: you leave as little as possible to chance.'

I handed the phone to Mrs Penzler. She switched it on and scrolled to the last text sent, then called the number. Muddy's phone started ringing and she cancelled the call. Then she gave Harry the iciest look I've ever seen. I'm sure teachers get trained to do that.

'I expect this phone was only bought a couple of days ago,' I said, trying not to shiver at the sight of Mrs Penzler's steely gaze. 'No doubt Harry was planning to destroy it, or its SIM card at least, as soon as he was safely outside the school again. Then that text he sent would have been untraceable.'

By now, the rain had started pounding again. We all made our way back towards the assembly hall. Muddy, Izzy and I got ready to leave, looking glumly out at the gushing skies. Izzy flapped her umbrella into shape, and I turned up the collar of my coat. Harry Lovecraft just stood there, staring viciously at us.

'You three will need to talk to the Head about this on Monday morning,' said Mrs Penzler. 'Harry and I will see her as soon as the conference is over. Try not to get too wet on the way home. Oh, and Saxby . . .'

'Yes?' I said, turning back at the open door.

'Where on earth did you get that awful raincoat?' asked Mrs Penzler. 'You look like a giant gherkin.'

The Head suspended Harry Lovecraft immediately. A few days later it turned out that he'd stolen his latest stepmother's credit card to pay online for the phone and all the stuff he'd used in that smoke grenade. His dad, after finally persuading the Head not to get the police involved, moved Harry to another school about twenty miles away. With luck, I thought, I'll never see him again.

I arrived back at my garden shed wet and weary. I hung up my lovely, keeps-you-warm, attractive-shade-of-green raincoat, and flopped into my Thinking Chair.

I was about to start noting down a few facts about the case when I heard a *plip-plip-plip* coming from the corner. Oh . . . bottoms. I'd forgotten about that leak in the roof.

The paint tin I'd placed under the drip was now almost full. With a deep sigh, I picked it up, stuck my arm out of the shed door and emptied the tin out on to the lawn.

I glared up at the leak. Hmm. I was going to have to do something about that.

Case closed.

74

CASE FILE SEVENTEEN:

MARCH OF THE ZOMBIES

CHAPTER ONE

OK. STAY CALM. DON'T PANIC.

I took a deep breath. Then I took another deep breath.

I was *determined* to get this right. There was a leak in the roof of my shed, my Crime HQ, and I was absolutely *determined* to solve the problem on my own.

The rain, which had been bucketing down for days, had now stopped for a rest. However, from the look of the sky, it would start chucking down all over the place again just as soon as the clouds had gathered enough water again to chuck.

So I didn't have long. I'm a brilliant schoolboy detective but I'm totally hopeless when it comes to practical things like making 3D models for school projects, or doing toast without any burned bits, or mending leaks in sheds. I was fed up of getting this sort of thing wrong so I was *determined* that this particular little job would be done properly. Without botching it. And without leaving tatty patches.

For advice, I'd turned to my friend George 'Muddy' Whitehouse, St Egbert's School's Crown Prince of Engineering. He'd told me exactly what tools and equipment I'd need to repair the shed, and he'd taken me through doing the job step-by-step.

'You sure you don't want me to do it for you?' he'd asked, covered in grease as he adapted an old bike into a go-cart. 'You know what you're like with these things.'

'No,' I said firmly. 'Thank you, no. I'm going to do this myself and I'm going to get it right. I'm *determined*.'

'Fair enough,' said Muddy with a shrug.

I'd felt very confident after I'd talked to Muddy. However, now I was back in my shed and staring up at the wet patch in the corner of the roof, I was feeling rather nervous.

Now the rain was having a tea break, water was no longer plipping from the roof into the old paint tin I'd placed on my filing cabinet full of case notes. It was time to begin.

I checked my equipment: hammer, large scissors, little silver nails with a big flat bit at the top, roofing felt (thick wobbly sheet stuff, dark grey on one side, gritty green on the other). Check! Instructions: cut roofing felt to size, place over leaking area, nail down around the edge. Check!

Half an hour later, I was done.

And it looked pretty good! I gazed up at the neat rectangle of roofing felt I'd nailed into place directly above the filing cabinet and I was overjoyed. I almost hopped up and down with delight!

A-ha! Do your worst, rain! I thought as I sat down victoriously in my Thinking Chair.

At that moment, there was a knock on the shed door. 'C'min!' I cried.

In came a short, thin boy with close-cropped hair and an expression of mild dislike. He was wearing baggy jeans and a chunky pullover which looked like it had been knitted from blue spaghetti. His face was round and small with a nose like a mushroom. I'd never seen him before.

'Are you Saxby Smart?' he said. His eyes flicked around the shed, glancing across the piles of gardening and DIY stuff. He didn't seem impressed by my desk, or my filing cabinet, or even my Thinking Chair, the battered old leather armchair in which I've puzzled out many a mystery.

'That's me!' I beamed. I pointed up to the new patch on the ceiling. 'Look. I did that.' I nodded eagerly at him and grinned.

'Er . . . great,' he said. 'My name's Luke. Luke Dixon. You're a detective, right?'

'A detective, and Highly Skilled Leaky Roof Repairer, yes,' I said. 'How can I help you? You're not at St Egbert's?'

'No, I live across town,' said Luke. 'I know Danielle Plummley. She said you'd got her out of trouble once.'

Danielle was in my class at school. I'd been able to help her out on the school trip to Paris (see Volume Three of my case files). 'What's the problem?' I said, ushering Luke to my Thinking Chair while I perched on the desk.

I was about to encounter a crime which had a strange and unusual motive. This case would leave me thinking serious thoughts about why people do what they sometimes do.

'Well, it's not me that's got the problem,' said Luke. 'It's my friend's dad's brother's next-door neighbour.'

'Uh-huh.' I nodded. 'So, why isn't it your friend's dad's brother's next-door neighbour who's coming to see me?'

'The cops have got him locked up,' said Luke. 'He's under arrest.'

'What for?' I asked.

'Stealing one hundred and thirty thousand copies of a new video game,' said Luke calmly.

80

CHAPTER
TWO

'*HOW* MANY?!' I GASPED.

'It was the entire contents of one medium-sized truck,' said Luke. 'One hundred and thirty thousand games. Well, one hundred and twenty-nine thousand nine hundred and ninety-six, to be exact.'

'And why is he a suspect?' I asked.

'Because it looks like he did it,' said Luke. 'He had a reason to steal those games, he had the ability to steal them and he had a perfect chance to steal them.'

I hmmmed for a moment. 'Correct me if I'm on the wrong track, here,' I said, 'but doesn't that mean he's probably guilty?'

'That's the whole point,' said Luke. 'He isn't. He's been framed, stitched up, made a fall guy.'

'What makes you so sure? If he had a motive, a method *and* an opportunity, he'd be at the top of my suspect list, I can tell you that.'

'Because he doesn't want to go to prison,' said Luke. 'Not again. He's only just got out!'

If I'd been drinking a glass of water at that moment, I'd have sprayed it out across the shed in a shower of surprise. However, I wasn't, so I didn't.

'He's got a motive, a method, an opportunity, *and* he's committed crimes in the past!' I spluttered. 'Look, Luke, I don't want to sound heartless but surely it's a defence lawyer he needs, not a detective? And a defence lawyer who specialises in defending hopeless cases, at that!'

'My friend's dad's brother knows this guy well,' said Luke. 'He swears on his life that someone's framing him.'

'How does your friend's dad's brother know him?' I asked.

'They were in prison together.'

If my eyebrows had risen any higher, they'd have missed my head completely. 'This gets better and better,' I said. 'Not only does this guy look totally guilty, but the person who's most on his side is another villain!'

Luke sighed. 'I know it looks bad. But will you hear the full story first and then make up your mind?'

He was right. I was jumping to conclusions. What

kind of detective would I be if I formed an opinion before knowing all the facts? A rubbish one, that's what! I felt embarrassed. (My spectacular success at roof repairing must have gone to my head.)

'Let's fill in all the details,' I said. 'OK. First, this video game.'

'What's been stolen,' said Luke, in a deadly serious tone, 'is the entire UK supply of *March of the Zombies 3*.' He seemed to be expecting me to start leaping around, tearing my hair out and shouting, 'Oh no! Not *March of the Zombies 3*! It can't be true! Nooooooo!'

I stared blankly at him. 'What's that, then?'

'You've never played *March of the Zombies 2*?' he gasped.

'I've never played *March of the Zombies 1*,' I told him.

Luke shook his head sadly. 'Yeah, Danielle said you're strangely out of touch.'

'Did she, now.'

'Yeah. *March of the Zombies* is, like, the best zombie shoot-'em-up franchise *ever*. Part 3 is set on a space station. It's supposed to go on sale next Friday at 9 a.m., and until then it's strictly under wraps. Nobody is allowed a copy and the shops that will be selling it won't get their supplies until the Thursday afternoon. That medium-sized truck I mentioned was taking the whole launch-day supply from a ship, which docked somewhere on the south coast, up to the distribution depot that's near the shopping mall – Dales Road Haulage & Transport Ltd.'

'One medium-sized truck?' I said. 'Surely a quantity that huge would take up a couple of whopping great articulated lorries at least?'

I tried doing a few calculations in my head to work out the volumes involved. My head didn't like that idea at all. So I quickly gave up.

'Yes,' said Luke, 'one hundred and twenty-nine thousand nine hundred and ninety-six games would take up half a warehouse. But *March of the Zombies 3* was being shipped disc-only, just as ordinary game discs in little plastic wallets, packed into boxes of thirty-six. The cases and instruction booklets and so on were going to be added at Dales. The covers for the UK edition have been printed in the UK, but the discs themselves have to be imported from China.'

'Even so,' I said, 'that number of discs must take up a lot of space. Let's see . . . if a disc, in a little plastic wallet, is about, umm, a hundred and thirty millimetres square, and about three millimetres thick, that means . . . umm . . . er . . .'

I reached into my desk and took out a pocket calculator. 'One thirty . . . times one thirty . . .' I mumbled, tapping at keys, 'times three, times the number of copies

. . . no, I need to do that in metres, don't I . . . umm . . .'

The calculation for working out the total volume that all those discs would occupy was 0.13m x 0.13m x 0.03m x 129,996. I'm sure you can find the answer faster than I could . . .

'A-ha!' I cried at last. Then I squinted at the calculator. 'Hang on, this is the size of a pizza box, that can't be right.'

Tutting, Luke took the calculator from me and worked it out for himself.

'Yeah, Danielle said you're surprisingly dodgy at maths,' commented Luke.

'Did she, now,' I said. 'I'm rapidly going off her.'

Luke finished tapping out numbers. 'The total volume is 65.9 cubic metres. Yeah, it's a lot, but that's still less than an average classroom.'

I hmmm-ed again. Something still bothered me.

'If you have thirty-six discs to a box,' said Luke, 'that's [*tap tap tap*] about a hundred and fifty boxes per pallet, that's [*tap tap tap*] only about twenty-five pallets.'

'What's a pallet?' I asked.

'It's like a flat wooden platform, about a metre and a half across. You see them in warehouses being moved around with forklift trucks. Things get stacked on to them, then they're often wrapped around with that kind of giant-sized cling film.'

'Ah, yes, I know what you mean,' I said. 'You know a lot about this . . .'

'My friend's dad works for Dales Ltd. He took us over there to have a look around once, on a Sunday when nobody was working. It's a big place.'

'And they import things from abroad?' I asked.

'Quite often,' said Luke. 'Companies hire them to collect large quantities of whatever, and then deliver them, either to high street shops or to other depots. They mail out stuff for online shops, too. They do games, toys, electrical goods, books, furniture, all sorts.'

'So this truck-load was a routine job?' I asked.

'Yes, except that it was supposed to be secret,' replied Luke. 'Gamers have been itching to get their mitts on *March of the Zombies 3* for months so Dales had to promise the software developers that they'd keep the discs under lock and key until next week. They weren't even going to tell their staff until next week that they were handling the game. The only people who knew that *March of the Zombies 3* was arriving were the owner of the company, Len Dale, his son Stephen Dale, who runs the company's office, and the truck driver who was collecting the discs, a man called Peter Lyndon.'

'I see,' I said. 'So how did your friend's dad's brother's next-door neighbour get to hear about it?'

'He's Peter Lyndon.'

'Ah.'

'Yes, he works for my friend's dad, who's a supervisor. This Peter Lyndon was only hired by Dales about a month ago. He'd been in prison for a couple of years. He'd stolen a security van full of cash when the driver hopped out to have a wee. People who've been in that sort of trouble have problems finding a job, as you can imagine, but Len Dale had signed up for a government scheme which helps ex-prisoners. Peter Lyndon was a qualified truck driver so Dales was an ideal place to work.'

'And he was given the job of transporting *March of the Zombies 3,*' I said, jotting a few things down in my notebook.

'Yes, the night before last,' said Luke. 'It was done late at night because the delivery was so secret. The truck was due to get back to Dales at about one in the morning. Len Dale arrived next day and found that the truck hadn't returned. When Stephen Dale turned up for work a few minutes later, Len got him to check the truck's location.'

'They have a system for pinpointing their vehicles?' I asked.

'Yes, some sort of sat-nav thing,' said Luke. 'They found out that the truck was on a road a couple of miles outside town. Then Len Dale and a couple of workers from the depot – including my friend's dad – went out to see what had happened. They found a field covered in tyre tracks, where the truck must have been unloaded. The truck itself had been abandoned a few hundred metres further on, hidden away behind a farm building, out of sight of the road. It was empty and there was no sign of where the games could have gone.'

'So where was the driver, Peter Lyndon?'

'Well, at that point, Len Dale called the police,' said Luke. 'He was worried that whoever dumped the truck had dumped Peter Lyndon too. The police called at Lyndon's house —'

'Next door to your friend's dad's brother,' I prompted.

'That's right. Lyndon was at home. He said he'd been given the day off by Dales because he'd worked late the night before. Which was perfectly true. He said he'd driven the truck to Dales, as arranged. He said he knew nothing about the missing discs.'

'Aren't there security cameras at Dales, to back up his story?' I asked.

'There are cameras, but the recorder broke months ago. Dales have never had a problem like this before and they just never got round to having it fixed.'

'And there wasn't any kind of log of Peter arriving at the depot with the truck, or anyone else there?' I said.

He shook his head.

'So the police didn't believe what Lyndon said?'

'No. They thought he'd stopped the truck in that field, then called in a load of criminal, underworld-type ex-convict friends to help unload everything. Then, with the discs whisked off by his mates, he'd dumped the truck and walked home. The police said that this was clearly what Lyndon had planned because it left him in a his-word-against-Dales situation. His helpers had taken away all the evidence. He could sit there and say "Nothing to do with me, mate". The police searched his house, but didn't find anything relevant.'

I hmmmed yet again. Another something was bothering me. 'You said before that he had a motive. I can't really see one.'

'What? The money he and his mates would make from selling the games, obviously!' exclaimed Luke. 'Even if he sold them at one pound each, he'd make a huge pile of cash! And they're worth a lot more than a pound.'

'But no matter how strong your motive for committing a crime might be,' I said, 'you won't actually commit it unless you thought you'd got a fair chance of getting away with it. Why would you steal something if you knew you were going to be top of the suspect list?'

Luke wrinkled his nose up. 'The police say he's trying to bluff his way out of it. They don't have firm evidence against him yet, remember. That's why they're still questioning him. They're trying to get him to reveal who his thieving partners-in-crime are.'

'Bluff his way out of it?' I pondered, mostly to myself. 'That's a risky idea.'

'Everyone at Dales is really upset,' said Luke. 'My friend's dad says Lyndon seemed like a nice chap who was trying to put his past behind him. Len Dale is upset because he personally hired Lyndon and he feels his trust has been betrayed. Stephen Dale is upset because the software company behind *March of the Zombies 3* is never likely to use Dales again.'

'What happens if the discs aren't found?' I asked. 'Will Dales end up owing the software company a lot of money?'

'I don't know,' said Luke. 'I guess so. It's the breach of security they're more worried about at the moment. You see, they can't work out *how* someone outside Dales found out about the discs. So they're coming to the same conclusion as the police: that Lyndon must be lying. But he's not. He delivered that truck to Dales, just as he said he did. That's where you come in. You have to prove that someone, somewhere, somehow, knew those discs were on their way to Dales and that they've framed Lyndon for the theft.'

Luke paused. He shuffled forwards on my Thinking Chair. 'Well, those are the facts. What do you think?'

'I think there's more to this mystery than first meets the eye,' I said. 'Saxby Smart is on the case!'

A Page From My Notebook

I need to be careful. So far, it's perfectly possible that the police are right, that Luke is wrong, and that this Peter Lyndon really DID do it. I must keep an OPEN MIND. However, there are some puzzling things about this case:

PUZZLING THING 1: If Lyndon DID do it, then WHY? He MUST have known the police would come straight to his door. He'd have to be crazy to think they wouldn't. Or . . . maybe he IS crazy?

PUZZLING THING 2: If Lyndon DIDN'T do it, we're left with a couple of problems. FIRST: the thieves must have removed the truck from Dale's – after Lyndon had driven it back to the depot at one in the morning – and taken it to that field. WHY? Why not just unload it at Dale's? SECOND: If they took the truck from Dale's, why unload it AT ALL? Why not just disable the sat-nav locator-thingy, and steal the truck too? Why bother swapping trucks?

PUZZLING THING 3: Despite what Luke said, those discs DO take up a large amount of space. WHERE could you hide that amount of stuff? It's not like you could sneak it under the sofa and hope nobody will notice!

Important Question: Is it TRUE that only Len Dale, Stephen Dale and Peter Lyndon knew about the delivery of discs?

If the answer to the question is NO . . .

• Did someone else at Dale's know? If so, HOW?

• Did someone from the software company arrange the robbery? If so, WHY?

• Did someone else entirely find out? If so, WHO?

And if the answer to the question is YES . . . then Peter Lyndon definitely looks guilty, because Len and Stephen Dale certainly have nothing to gain from the crime. Which brings us back full circle to PUZZLING THING 1 . . .

I think my brain just went phrrhhhtt.

CHAPTER
THREE

THERE WAS NO TIME TO lose. Luckily, we were in the middle of half-term week, so school wasn't a factor.

The first thing I did was phone my friend Isobel 'Izzy' Moustique, that well-known Commander of Cyberspace and Mayoress of Knowledge City. I gave her the basic facts of the case and asked her to dig up all she could on Dales and anything else she thought might be relevant. I arranged to meet up with her the following day.

The second thing I did was go and borrow a bike from Muddy. Luke had parked his bike at my garden gate – a really smart, shiny model in metallic blue, with an extended, arching mudguard at the back which looked like a tail streaming out behind a puma. It made my own

bike – a really grotty, scratched model in unsightly rust –
look a bit feeble. Using one of Muddy's specially
modified vehicles would look far more detectivey. (Plus,
my bike had only one wheel. And it was slightly bent.
And I wasn't even sure where I'd left it.)

I'd decided to take a look at the crime scene – the field
where the truck had been unloaded. Luke went on
ahead, while I hurried over to Muddy's house. He was
busy in his garage (or Development Laboratory, as he
prefers to call it), putting the finishing touches to a
device for seeing around corners. As always, his clothes
were almost as covered in grime and food stains as his
face.

'You could borrow that go-cart,' said Muddy. 'Just
finished. Twelve gears.'

'No thanks,' I said. 'I want to look cool and
detectivey.'

'It's got a really stylish curved section at the front,' he
said, with a grin. 'Makes it look a bit like a car.'

'Thanks, no, just the bike.'

He pulled an OK-please-yourself face. 'You can have
the *Whitehouse SpeedMaster 5000*, over there in the corner.
But it's not as trendy as that go-cart, I'm telling you.'

Half an hour later, I'd cycled out of town, along a
long, curving road which skirted the area beyond the bus
station and the shopping mall. To one side of the road

were lines of tall trees, swaying and swishing in the wind. On the other side was a series of squarish fields, marked out with scrappy hedges, one or two of them accessible from the road through broad metal gates.

By the time I caught up with Luke, I was totally exhausted. One of these days I really *must* start to get more exercise.

'What kept you?' asked Luke.

'I was . . . er . . .' I gasped, wheeling to a stop and trying to catch my breath.

Luke propped his bike up against a hedge. 'Yeah, Danielle said you're surprisingly unfit.'

'Did she, now,' I wheezed.

'This is the field,' said Luke. 'You can see there are loads of tyre tracks coming in and out past the gate.'

I left the *Whitehouse SpeedMaster 5000* next to Luke's bike and walked across soft, rutted grass into the field. I walked quite slowly, partly to examine the tracks and partly to recover from all that cycling.

As Luke had spotted, there were deep, overlapping lines of tracks by the gates. All the tyre marks were the same: wide, chunky and obviously made by something large. Past the gate, the tracks spread out into a wildly criss-crossed pattern. The ground was still quite damp from all the recent rain and had been mashed into a brown and bumpy paste. Here and there, a few lonely blades of grass clung together, like shipwrecked sailors on a sea of mud.

All the indentations in the ground were clear and fresh. I tried to make sense of them, following one track after another, to see if I could piece together the sequence of events from the way the tracks twisted and turned.

'What can you deduce?' called Luke from the gate.

'Very little,' I cried, taking a big step over a patch where half a dozen lines appeared to cross each other. 'I don't understand this at all. With tyre tracks, you can always tell which were made last because they go over the top of the others —'

'Yeah, that makes sense,' said Luke.

'But these seem to go all over the place. They look so similar, I can't be definite about anything at all.'

Feeling frustrated, I glanced back at the route I'd taken around the field. Heavy tyre tracks formed a large, tree-like pattern in the mud, and through the middle of it all were the oval shapes of my own shoes as I'd tiptoed about.

'On second thoughts,' I said, 'there *is* something I can be definite about.'

'What?' called Luke.

'Clearly, that truck *was* here,' I cried. 'But I don't think it was unloaded. Not in this field.'

'Huh?' called Luke. 'What makes you say that? What have you seen?'

'It's what I haven't seen that's the important thing,' I said.

Have you worked it out too? Can you spot the missing element?

'Look all around here,' I called over to Luke. 'Heavy vehicle tracks. And what else?'

'Er, nothing,' said Luke.

'Exactly! I've just walked around this field and left a clear line of footprints. A truck is supposed to have been unloaded here in the middle of the night, by this bunch of crooks Peter Lyndon is supposed to have organised. So how come there's not a single one of their footprints anywhere? The police must have only *looked* in the field.'

Luke frowned, then stared, then frowned again. 'Huh? That doesn't make sense! Why would anyone drive the truck in here and *not* unload it? Hey, wait a minute, if the truck wasn't unloaded that means Lyndon is telling the truth, right?'

I hopped over the mud, back to where Luke was standing. 'No, what it means is that the story the police and Dales have put together is wrong. As far as this field goes anyway.'

'So, which version of events is right then?'

'I haven't the faintest idea,' I said. 'Yet.'

'What do we do now?' said Luke, swinging himself back on to his bike.

I thought for a moment. 'Your friend's dad, the one who works at Dales. Do you think he could get us in there, right now, to have a look around? Using a cover story, of course, so that nobody else would know we're investigating the robbery.'

'Dunno,' said Luke. 'Probably, if it'll help solve the case. I'll phone my friend, he can ask for us.'

Luke quickly made arrangements. Then, suddenly, I had a thought which set my heart thumping, a thought which made my head spin and my legs go weak: going over to Dales would mean another long bike ride.

CHAPTER
FOUR

DALES ROAD HAULAGE & TRANSPORT LTD was a big place.
Really, really, big. *Biiiig!*

Beyond a high metal fence was a row of enormous,
warehouse-style buildings, each of which could easily
have fitted the whole of St Egbert's School into it. Twice.
A small, two-storey office block stuck out in front of the
first building and it was here that Luke and I were met by
his friend's dad, who turned out to be called Reg Pratt.

Mr Pratt was a rosy-cheeked, gravelly-voiced man,
who blinked a lot and had a habit of tugging at his nose
every now and then. He wore blue overalls with *Dales
Ltd* sewn across the back in large yellow letters.

'Right then, lads,' he said, in a broad Welsh accent, as
he led us towards the nearest warehouse, 'remind me

again, what are you pretending to be here for?'

'The St Egbert's School newspaper,' I said. 'We're doing a project called *Important Things in our Community*.'

'Right then,' said Mr Pratt. 'You tell me what you want to see, and I'll pretend you're doing a project and not investigating those stolen games.'

'Excellent,' I said. 'Let's take a look at the truck.'

As the three of us entered the building, I was wowed by three things: its size, its noise and its temperature. Even though I'd been impressed by the hugeness of these warehouses from the outside, the sight of the inside impressed me all over again. The place was alive with bumps, clangs, shouts, beeps, mechanical whirrs, and here and there the squawk of a radio. It was also very cold.

Part of the vast floorspace was occupied by long, machinery-covered benches, at which rows of people were sorting DVDs into piles, or filling padded envelopes ready to mail out. Most of the rest was filled, floor to ceiling, with chunky metal racking, on which were stacked thousands of crates, boxes and cartons. Forklift trucks buzzed about, orange warning lights flashing on top of them. Just visible, right at the far end of the warehouse, was a line of trucks parked in front of a series of big, roll-up metal doors.

'This is where items like books and DVDs get processed and despatched,' explained Mr Pratt, raising his voice above the din. He suddenly snapped his fingers and pointed to a forklift that was gliding close by, ferrying a pallet piled with cardboard boxes. It set the pallet down by the nearest bench, where a spotty-faced worker started unloading the boxes.

'Ah, perfect timing!' cried Mr Pratt, hurrying us across to the bench. I saw that the cardboard boxes each had a video game cover sticky-taped over them. Printed on the covers, in drippy, blood-red letters was *March of the Zombies 3 – The Undead are BACK, and this time they're IN A RIGHT STROP!*

'Right then, Geoff,' said Mr Pratt, 'when did these arrive?'

''Bout ten minutes ago,' sniffed the spotty-faced worker. 'Len wants me to check 'em and store 'em down here. He's hoping the discs get found soon, then we can get cracking and still make the delivery deadline next week.'

'These two lads here,' said Mr Pratt, 'are from St Ethel's School. They're doing a project called *Interesting Thoughts of a Committee.* Nothing to do with the stolen games.'

'H'lo.' Geoff nodded at us.

I groaned to myself. Mr Pratt led us away, in the direction of the trucks.

'Is it usual for you to have to package-up video games like that?' I asked.

'No, we only need to do it now and again,' said Mr Pratt. 'Normally, games come in fully packaged, in their cases, with covers, and so on. But there was a shocking mix-up on *March of the Zombies 2*. All the covers of the overseas editions got mistranslated as *March of the Poo-Poo-Bum-Bums*. That's why the software company is being extra careful about everything this time. All the overseas covers are being printed and checked separately.'

'But the discs are coming from China?' I said.

'That's right,' said Mr Pratt. 'They're all being made at a factory in Shanghai. That stolen truck-load was a special order.'

'What was special about it?' I asked.

'*March of the Zombies 3* is being released in this country three months ahead of the rest of the world,' Luke replied.

'Why?' I said.

'Dunno,' said Luke. 'Some sales gimmick, I guess. Gamers can't wait to get their hands on it.'

'So the stolen discs are the only copies of the game that currently exist?' I said.

'For the time being, yes,' agreed Mr Pratt. 'Right then, here we are, here's part of our fleet of vehicles.'

We'd arrived at the line of parked trucks. There must have been at least two dozen of them. Some were quite small, but some were giant, road-hogging lorries with wheels as tall as the average car. As we stood there, another one pulled up at the far end of the row, with a hiss of brakes and a roar of its engine.

One of the medium-sized trucks instantly caught my attention. It looked quite new, but was road-grubby. A manky-looking toy mouse was tied to its radiator grille.

'A-ha!' I cried. 'You don't have to be a brilliant schoolboy detective like me to spot the vital clue here. Notice the mud pressed into the tyres, which have the same pattern as the tracks left in the field. And [*sniff, sniff*] the mud smells the same as that field, too. Yes, I can definitely say without a shadow of a doubt that this is the truck which was used to transport the discs.'

'No, it's this one over here,' called Mr Pratt, from further down the line of vehicles.

'Oh,' I said quietly. I scurried over to the correct truck. Ah, apparently all Dales' medium-sized trucks were, umm, the same model, er, and they used the, er, same type of tyres. Easy mistake, a-hem a-hem.

The correct truck was a little older and even more in need of a wash. The mud on its tyres smelled the same, though.

'The police examined it in detail,' said Mr Pratt, 'but they found no lead on where the discs might have gone.'

We took a good look inside the truck and around the driver's cabin, but I found nothing unexpected or unusual. I was feeling disappointed as Mr Pratt led Luke and me back to the depot's offices. I'd been hoping that an examination of the truck would turn up one or two clues.

As we walked away from the long line of vehicles, I happened to glance back. All the trucks were dusty and grimy from use, but only those two medium-sized ones had muddy tyres. I pulled my notebook from my pocket and jotted down an observation.

In contrast to the warehouses, the main office at Dales was unusually cosy. Two secretaries were tapping away on computers at one end of the long, rectangular room. At the other end, in front of a broad window which overlooked the depot, was a larger desk which was occupied by a timid-looking man wearing a suit which didn't suit him. The office was warm and carpeted, and around the walls were various charts and paper-dotted noticeboards.

'Right then, Stephen,' said Mr Pratt to the timid-looking man as he ushered us into the room, 'these two lads with me here are the boys from St Elsie's School I said were visiting. They're doing a project on *Invertebrate Things on a Calculator*.'

'Nice to meet you,' said Stephen Dale, standing up and shaking our hands.

Mr Pratt stepped forward and spoke to Stephen Dale in a low voice. 'They're not investigating those stolen games, or anything like that,' he said, wagging a finger.

Stephen chuckled. 'Well, no, you're hardly likely to find a schoolboy investigating a serious crime, now, are you?'

We all had a good laugh about that one, ha ha ha. Quickly, I said, 'You've got a very impressive place here, Mr Dale. How do you keep track of it all?'

'It's all controlled from my computer, right here on my desk,' said Stephen. 'Every movement of every vehicle, and every item on every shelf out in the warehouses, gets listed and catalogued by me personally.'

At that moment, Len Dale entered the office. He was tall and bald, with a hawkish, wrinkled face. He was clearly having a bad day. I wondered if it had anything to do with the fact that his suit was even worse than Stephen's.

'Hi Dad,' said Stephen. 'These are our visitors from St Ermintrude's School. They're doing a project on *Invisible Things in a Cauliflower*.'

'Good to see you, boys,' said Len Dale, his face less cheery than his words. 'We like to do our bit for the community. Although the way things have been going, I'm rapidly starting to re-think that idea.'

'I'm giving them a tour,' said Mr Pratt. 'They're not investigating those missing games.'

Len Dale snorted. 'I almost wish they were. The police don't seem to be making any progress with that jailbird Lyndon. Any news, Steve?'

'No, sorry, Dad,' said Stephen glumly. 'I called them

earlier and they're still questioning him. They'll have to let him go some time tomorrow if no evidence turns up or he doesn't confess.'

Len sighed, shaking his head in dismay. 'You place your trust in someone, you try to help them out, and they stab you in the back.' He suddenly winced. 'Ohh! Talking of backs, mine's still killing me.'

'That'll be stress, that will,' said Mr Pratt. 'It's been hurting you since this robbery came to light, yes? Stress does terrible damage to the human body, you know.'

Len turned to me and Luke. 'Boys, you'll have to forgive us, this is a difficult time for Dales. Clearly, our Mr Pratt has told you why that is, but I do hope your project will include all the positive aspects of our business instead. I expect you'll want to interview me now? I see you've got a notebook there, son.'

I glanced at Luke. 'Er, yes, right, definitely,' I said.

Len Dale launched himself into a speech, like an ocean liner being launched on a trans-Atlantic voyage. 'I started this company thirty-two years ago,' he began. 'All I had in those days was a tin shack and a wheelbarrow . . . Are you writing this down? . . . A tin shack, a wheelbarrow and a love of road transport . . .'

Two hours later, I arrived back home. I had a slight headache and seventeen pages of almost-useless notes on Len Dale's love of road transport.

A Page From My Notebook

(One that's not about road transport.)

OBSERVATION: Why did those TWO trucks have identical mud on their tyres? None of the other trucks' tyres were muddy. Were BOTH of them in that field? Or is the mud on the other truck simply a coincidence?

Thinking back to Len's earlier comment about trust: A question now occurs to me – why was Peter Lyndon sent to pick up those discs and not one of the other drivers? That was a vitally important job. Peter Lyndon had only recently been hired and had a criminal history. Whatever Len Dale might say, would he really trust Lyndon THAT much? So soon? I'M SURE THIS IS SIGNIFICANT!

Note to self: Must buy a new notebook. This one's nearly full of notes on road transport.

CHAPTER FIVE

JUST AFTER BREAKFAST THE FOLLOWING day, I got a phone call from Luke. He said his mum had been driving past Dales at about nine thirty p.m. the night before, and had seen a light on in the office. I said I'd make a note of it, but it was probably just Len or Stephen working late.

I was wrong. Five minutes later, Luke called me again. He said his friend's dad, Mr Pratt, had just let him know that the Dales depot had been broken into overnight. I asked what had been taken. Even before Luke replied, I knew the answer: every last box with a cover for *March of the Zombies 3*. I shut my eyes and groaned.

The thieves were stepping up their plans! Everything they needed to sell *March of the Zombies 3* was entirely in their hands now.

That morning ended up divided into three short visits.

VISIT No. 1: Izzy's house.

Izzy was in her ultra-girlie, disco-coloured room. She swung around in her chair to face me, as I slumped awkwardly on to a beanbag. She brandished a set of computer print-outs.

'What have you found?' I asked, slowly toppling over to one side.

'Something very interesting,' replied Izzy. She plucked out a sheet of paper with a flick of her multi-ringed fingers. 'Dales is in big money trouble. They have been for a while.'

'Really?' I said, feeling my bottom sink lower and lower into the beanbag. 'They seemed pretty busy.'

'Not nearly as busy as they should be,' said Izzy. 'If you'd paid more attention to world news, you'd know that lots of businesses, big and small, are having a tough time right now. I've found articles from various sources which say Dales has got a major cash flow problem.'

'What's cash flow?' I asked.

She did that sarcastic arched-eyebrow-thing she does. (I can't duplicate it. If I try, I just look a bit startled.)

'Yeah, yeah,' I said, 'should pay more attention to the news, blah blah – what's cash flow?'

'Well, put it like this,' said Izzy, 'when you're running

a business, it's no good knowing you've got work coming in next month, if you need money to pay bills today. You have to make sure a certain minimum amount of money keeps coming into your business, just to keep the lights on, buy paper clips, all the basic stuff.'

'And Dales doesn't have enough money coming in?' I said.

'Right.'

'So this robbery could really hurt them.'

'Well, yes and no,' replied Izzy. 'Yes, because that software company isn't very likely to use Dales' services again. No, because Dales will almost certainly be insured against a crime like this.'

'How does that work?' I asked.

'Dales will have an insurance policy which will pay up if one of their deliveries is stolen or damaged. The software company will get the money that Dales *would* have owed them for all those discs, but it'll come from the insurance company.'

'So Dales' money problems won't get worse because of this robbery,' I said.

'Correct,' said Izzy. 'Which is lucky, because otherwise they might have had to close down. Do you want to hear another interesting fact I've dug up?'

'Yup,' I said, gradually sliding off the beanbag and on to the fluffy carpet.

'The software company, Bomb-Blast Games, is *also* having money problems. *March of the Zombies 3* is set to be their biggest game for years, but according to some of the internet gaming sites, they're having trouble raising enough cash to actually make the discs.'

'Ah!' I cried. 'That must be why they're releasing *March of the Zombies 3* in this country first. They need to sell as many as they can here so they can use the cash to make enough copies for the rest of the world.'

'Could be,' said Izzy.

I was now almost flat out on the floor. I struggled to my feet, and made a mental note to bring a chair with me next time.

'Thanks, Izzy,' I said. 'Gotta dash. See if you can find anything about where the stolen discs might turn up.'

'Will do,' said Izzy, doing a pretend salute.

VISIT No. 2: Peter Lyndon's house
Having no real evidence against him, the police were going to have to let Peter Lyndon go home. I'd arranged to meet Luke outside Lyndon's house before that happened, in case there were any clues to be had.

'But the cops searched the house when they arrested him,' said Luke, as our bikes slowed to a stop opposite a well-kept row of plain-fronted, 1970s-style houses. 'They didn't find anything.'

'They also thought the truck had been unloaded in that field,' I said. 'And they were wrong about that. I just want to gauge the size of Lyndon's house. We still have no idea where those hundreds of boxes are being stored.'

All along the street, the houses were arranged in pairs, like flipped-back-and-forth mirror images. Each had a large garage jutting out at the side. The houses themselves were quite small, but the garages were very broad – almost as wide as the houses – and taller than the average.

I gave Luke a hmm-*there's*-an-obvious-possibility look.

'Oh, don't be daft,' he spluttered. 'Surely the police checked the garage? Anyway, Lyndon's innocent! Those discs can't possibly be in there!'

We crossed the road and walked up the short, paved driveway in front of the garage. It was securely locked.

'I'm sure the police did check this garage,' I said. 'But I still want to check it myself.'

I got down on my hands and knees. I pressed my face against the driveway's surface so that I could peep into the two-centimetre gap under the bottom of the swing-up garage door.

A cold breeze stung at my eye. It took a few moments to adjust to the gloom inside, but I could soon tell that –

apart from a few gardening tools – the garage was empty.

Or was it?

'There's something on the floor,' I said, my voice squished from the peculiar angle my face was at. 'Scattered near this door. Looks like some pieces of paper, and something else, too.'

I poked my fingers into the gap. I couldn't reach very far, but the corner of the nearest sheet of paper was *just* touchable with my middle finger. I scraped at it carefully, pressing as hard as I could to get a grip.

Little by little, the paper shifted. I kept stopping to take another look into the gap. The paper was pulling some other stuff with it.

After a few minutes, the edge of a glossy white sheet slid into view. Delicately, so I didn't dislodge the stuff that was sitting on top of it, I pulled at the paper.

'Got it!' I cried.

What had been on top of the paper were three CD-sized plastic discs. Three discs with *March of the Zombies 3* printed on them. I turned the sheet of paper over. It was covered in drippy, blood-red lettering.

The Undead are BACK, and this time they're IN A RIGHT STROP!

'Oh no,' gasped Luke. 'Peter Lyndon *was* involved! He *did* plan the robbery – this proves it!'

'No,' I said, shaking my head, 'this proves the exact opposite. You were right, he's being framed. Someone wants to make sure that the police think he's guilty.'

'How can you be sure?' asked Luke.

I'd made a deduction. Have you spotted it too?

CHAPTER SIX

'THE POLICE FOUND NOTHING WHEN they arrested Lyndon,' I said. 'And there's no way they could have missed that stuff scattered on the garage floor. Therefore, it wasn't there when they searched. They've had Lyndon at the police station since then. So he couldn't possibly have had anything to do with these things being here – the thieves have only had these covers since last night.'

'But what if the thieves are using Lyndon's garage?' said Luke. 'He decoys the police, while they sneak in here?'

'What?' I cried. 'They move hundreds of boxes into this garage after it's been searched, then move it all out again the following night? No, it doesn't make sense. Someone has deliberately planted false evidence.'

'Someone who has the keys to his garage,' said Luke.

'Which still implies he's involved, somehow.'

As we re-crossed the road, back to our bikes, a police car purred into sight at the end of the street. There were two officers in the front seats and someone in the back I couldn't get a good look at.

'I bet that's Lyndon now,' said Luke. 'Nice of the cops to give him a lift home.'

I had a sudden, icy-cold feeling at the back of my neck. 'I don't think they're being kind,' I said quietly. 'I think whoever planted that evidence wants it to be found. I think the police have just had an anonymous tip-off and they're coming to search the house again.'

'They'll re-arrest him straightaway,' said Luke.

My phone rang. It was Izzy.

'Get back over here! Now!'

'Can't – something urgent's come up!' I told her.

'This is urgent too!' cried Izzy. 'Those games are being sold online, right now! Get here!'

The police car drew up outside Lyndon's house. The two officers got out, followed by a thin, scruffily-dressed man whose face displayed a mixture of embarrassment and anger.

'I've got to get to Izzy's,' I said. 'You stay here. Stop them.'

'Huh? *How?*'

'I've no idea. Just delay them, tell them what I've just told you, anything you like.'

I jumped on Muddy's bike and pedalled away as fast as I could. The situation was hotting up faster than a quick-boil kettle in a lava flow!

VISIT No. 3: Izzy's house again.
I stared at the screen of Izzy's computer, watching numbers tick rapidly left to right.

'What's this site called?' I said.

'Buy-Big-Bargains,' said Izzy. 'They're one of the largest auction sites. A seller has been offering copies of the game for auction since the early hours of this morning.'

There was a photo of one of the discs, boxed up and complete with cover. Across the screen, scrolling text declared: *Limited Time . . . 100% Genuine Stock, Imported Direct from Factory . . . Free Delivery Worldwide . . . Be First to Play MOTZ3 . . . Why Wait? Buy Direct . . . Buy Extra Copies for your Friends . . .*

'The crooks could have sold hundreds of those discs by now, if not thousands,' said Izzy. 'Each copy is going for about ten times what it would have cost in the shops. There are people from right around the world bidding!'

'Don't they know the discs are stolen?' I asked.

'Probably not,' replied Izzy. 'The robbery hasn't been front-page news, and certainly not across the rest of the planet. Even if some bidders do know, they probably don't care. There are plenty of people like that in the world.'

'Why doesn't the site just pull the auction?'

'If the games are genuine, which these are,' said Izzy, 'Buy-Big-Bargains won't do anything to interfere unless someone proves to them that stolen goods are involved. It's in their small print, their terms and conditions. The crooks have been very clever about it. It could take days to get this auction removed and by then the thieves will have sold half the truck-load.'

'What's the seller's name listed as?' I said. The screen flashed up another sale, and another, and another.

'The person everyone's paying is called Daphne Steel,' said Izzy. 'Her profile shows a five-star honesty rating *and* a five-star feedback rating *and* a five-star delivery rating. How, I have no idea. We have to assume the crooks have covered their tracks. We'll never trace them through this auction. Like I said, they've been very clever.'

I let out a sharp snort. 'Right, well, this Daphne Steel isn't the thief's real name, obviously.'

'Obviously.'

I gazed at the computer screen, watching helplessly as tick, tick, tick, tick, the stolen discs were bought for eye-bogglingly large sums of money.

What could I do? How could I stop this? How could I track the real crooks down? How could I show Peter Lyndon was innocent?

'Who'd give themselves an old-fashioned name like

Daphne?' muttered Izzy.

Izzy's words bounced around inside my head – and then, suddenly, they helped me spot the final clue. The last piece of the jigsaw. Everything became clear. Daphne Steel! I was so overjoyed I almost grabbed Izzy and kissed her. Luckily, I was able to stop myself in time!

'Daphne Steel!' I squeaked, leaping to my feet. 'I know what's been going on!'

I dashed out of the room. (I seem to have a habit of dashing out of Izzy's room . . .) I pounced on to Muddy's bike and rode off. I tried to steer with one hand and call Luke with the other. I ended up wobbling across the road and dropping the phone.

The whole case was made up of a surprisingly large number of different elements. Among the most intriguing were:

1. The name Daphne Steel.
2. The mud on the tyres of both those trucks.
3. Len Dale's backache.

How much of the puzzle have you pieced together?

CHAPTER
SEVEN

A COUPLE OF HOURS LATER, I was back at Dales Ltd. I stood in front of the long line of trucks at the back of the warehouse. Arranged in front of me, left to right, were Len Dale, Stephen Dale, Mr Pratt, Luke, Peter Lyndon and the two police officers who'd arrived at Lyndon's house.

The police officers were eyeing me suspiciously. One of them, a red-faced man with a chin like a house brick, was holding a see-through plastic bag containing *March of the Zombies 3* discs and covers, collected up from the floor of Peter Lyndon's garage.

'I've heard about you, Saxby Smart,' he growled quietly, 'from Inspector Godalming, back at the station. (See the case file *The Eye of the Serpent*.) 'We'll give you one chance to prove your case and if we're not convinced, we're arresting Mr Lyndon here on suspicion of theft. Again. Is that clear?'

'Completely,' I said. I tried not to show how nervous I was. Which wasn't easy because I was as nervous as a mouse at a cat show.

'OK,' I began. 'For a start, Peter Lyndon is innocent. He told the truth when he said that he collected those discs and delivered them here to Dales as arranged. You can all see the truck he used, parked over there.'

'Then how did the truck get into that field?' protested Len Dale.

'Once Lyndon had gone home,' I said, 'the truck was driven back out of here. It was then driven to the field, driven around the field and then dumped further down the road. A second truck went with it. This truck here, this one which *also* has mud from the field on its tyres. A second truck was taken out for two reasons. Firstly, because the field needed to have two distinct sets of tracks all over it if the police were going to believe that the first truck had been unloaded there. Secondly, because once the first truck was dumped, the driver would need a lift back here to the depot. The fact that two trucks were used that night showed me there were at least two people involved.'

'Hang on, hang on,' said Len Dale wearily. 'What on

earth was the point of doing all that? If someone was out to steal those discs, why not just take the truck from here?'

'Because the thieves needed to draw the police's attention away from themselves,' I said. 'The truck was dumped as part of a plot to frame Peter Lyndon. Someone drove two trucks all over that field, to make it look like the unloading had occurred there. But they forgot one detail. Footprints. They didn't leave any, so obviously the tyre tracks were only there to fool us. That's why I couldn't make sense of those tracks – I was looking for a logical pattern, and there wasn't one! But questions remained: Where *did* the discs get unloaded? Where *did* they go?'

'Well?' said one of the police officers.

'They *were* taken out of the first truck,' I said. 'They had to be, or the first truck couldn't have been dumped, empty at the side of the road. They *were* taken out of the first truck *and* put into the second truck. But none of that happened in the field. It happened right here, where we're standing. Why? Well, unloading and reloading all those boxes of discs would take a while, especially for just two people. And you'd ideally need a forklift. There'd be no point doing all that out in the open, where you might be seen. Not when you could do the unloading in here and stay safely hidden.'

'You're making a serious allegation there,' said the police officer. 'The only break-in there's been at Dales was last night. There was no break-in on the night the discs were stolen. If we're to believe your theory, all this truck-shifting business must have been carried out by persons with regular access to this depot. An inside job.'

'What?' said Len Dale. 'You're saying that two of our trusted employees did this? Then framed a third employee, Peter Lyndon here?'

'Sort of,' I said softly, my heart thumping, 'I'm saying that *you* did it, Mr Dale. You, and your son Stephen.'

Peter Lyndon had stayed silent and still until now. Now he turned sharply to stare in horror at Len and Stephen Dale. Len shook his head and tutted loudly.

'Oh really?' said Len, rocking slightly from foot to foot and crossing his arms. 'Stephen and I stole goods from our own business? When, instead, we could simply have distributed those discs to shops as normal and then made our normal profit from our normal business in the normal way? That makes sense, does it?'

'Well,' I said, 'it wouldn't make sense if Dales weren't in so much money trouble, no. But my guess is you know this company is going to close down soon so you seized an opportunity to pile up a large amount of cash for yourself, quickly, before it was too late. Your backache was a clue. All that re-loading would have been hard work, even using forklifts. You're an older man, if you don't mind my saying so, and naturally all that effort would have an effect. Of course, the backache isn't evidence, it could be nothing more than a coincidence, but it does fit into the overall picture.'

'And you think we'd do that, do you?' said Len Dale. He glared at me. 'We'd grab the money and run, is that it?'

'Dad . . .' murmured Stephen Dale.

The police officer tipped his cap back a bit on his head and scratched at his brick-like chin. 'What's this opportunity that got seized, then?'

'Dales is in deep trouble,' I said. 'If it closes down, its owners – the Dale family, Len Dale in particular – might lose everything. But a job turns up which presents a way to cushion the blow.

'Bomb-Blast Games, one of Dales' customers, are having troubles of their own. Their latest game, *March of the Zombies 3*, is likely to be a big hit worldwide, but they're short of cash. They decide to release the game in this country first, in order to build up enough cash to fund the release of the game everywhere else. They're being extra cautious. They're even having the game's covers printed separately.

'Dales are handling the game's distribution. And here's the opportunity that's waiting to be seized: it occurs to Len Dale that, when the discs arrive in the depot, Dales will have the entire world's supply of the game. A game which a lot of fans would pay well over the usual shop price for, if they could get their hands on it early.

'Dales couldn't exactly start selling copies on the sly. But suppose all those discs got stolen? There was literally a fortune to be made. Dales might be about to go under, but the Dale family could still come out ahead.

'Len and Stephen hatch a plan. They'll steal the discs, and get someone else blamed for the crime. So Len hires someone they can easily frame: someone who's just come out of prison, who's not only got a criminal record, but a record which includes robbery from a vehicle too. Peter Lyndon was perfect for them.

'Suspiciously perfect, in fact. From my point of view, at least. But the idea of the plan was to make sure that the police would focus on the clear and obvious suspect, while the guilty ones got on with the rest of their scheme. The police would be convinced that Lyndon, and a bunch of partners in crime, were the ones responsible. And if, in the end, there wasn't enough evidence to put him back in prison, it didn't really matter too much. By then the discs would be long gone and Len and Stephen would have their stash of cash and the police would still be watching Lyndon, waiting for him to make a slip-up and reveal "the truth". In the meantime, Dales' insurance cover would settle the bill with the software company, since the police were on the case and a suspect had already been arrested.

'So the discs are missing and Lyndon is being questioned at the police station. Move ahead a day or so, and now Dales has had the game's cover delivered. Len and Stephen need that too if they're going to sell the complete game as totally genuine, so they fake a break-in at this depot and steal the covers as well.

'The same night, last night, two other things happen: first, they put the selling part of their plan into operation. I'll get to that in a minute. Second, they plant evidence at Peter Lyndon's house so that when the police release him he gets re-arrested and diverts the police's attention for another couple of days. The planted evidence would back up the police's suspicion that Lyndon was working with others.'

'We've got Peter Lyndon's house keys, have we?' said Len Dale.

'You didn't need them,' I said. 'You could fling a few copies of the game and its cover into the small gap under the door of the garage. It would only take a minute.

'While Len is planting that evidence, Stephen is back here in the office setting up an online auction for the games and packaging up a load of games ready to mail.

The office lights are seen from a passing car, by the way. He uploads a photo to show the world that it's buying the real thing. The plastic cases for putting the discs and covers in, and all the envelopes for mailing, are stuff that can easily be supplied from the Dales warehouse. They do mail-outs for customers regularly, after all.

'The online auction begins late last night, and is continuing as I speak, run under the name of one Daphne Steel. Each copy of *March of the Zombies 3* is going for several times its regular price, so only a couple of thousand copies will need to be sold to amass a fortune. And then, once the games have been packaged up in secret, possibly during the night, they can be anonymously slipped into the hundreds of deliveries that leave this depot every day.

'By the time the Buy-Big-Bargains website has shut the auction down and the police have finally accepted that Lyndon knows nothing, it's too late. The discs that have been sold are on their way around the world. Len and Stephen have erased anything linking them to the mysterious Daphne Steel. The remaining discs can then be "found" somewhere. Oh, look, the crooks have abandoned them! Oh, goody, we can supply shops with the game after all! Oh, isn't that lovely, everything's turned out OK. If *only* there were some clue to the identity of those naughty robbers, eh? Tut, tut, never mind, thanks for your help, officer. No, you can be sure we'll sack that Lyndon character, can't trust him at all!'

'I've had enough of this nonsense,' growled Len Dale. 'You haven't a shred of proof, this is all just a wild theory.'

Stephen stood there silently, his face flushed a shade of red that a beetroot would be proud of. Peter Lyndon gaped horrified at the pair of them.

'Len Dale is quite correct,' said the police officer. 'At the moment, this is all just theory. How do we know this online auction is linked to the accused here?'

'There was one little detail which unlocked this whole case for me,' I explained. 'The mysterious Daphne Steel. Until I came across her, nothing seemed to fit properly.'

'Who is she then?' piped up Luke.

'She's a fake identity who's been constructed very cleverly and with great care,' I said. 'Except in one small respect. Perhaps this one weak spot was simply the result of a moment's carelessness. Or maybe a mistaken belief that the connection wouldn't be spotted.'

'What connection?' said the police officer, scratching his chin again.

'Her name,' I said. 'Daphne Steel is an anagram of Stephen Dale.'

All seven people in front of me did a double-take. Both police officers looked over at the Dales. Len and Stephen Dale went slightly pale. Peter Lyndon and Luke looked like they'd been slapped in the face with a wet fish. Mr Pratt just looked bewildered.

'Mind you,' I said, 'that's still not proof. It could still be the case that some other employee of this company set that ID up to frame Stephen. A kind of frame within a frame! But, like Len's backache, you put it all together and the overall picture becomes clear. Especially when you realise where the discs have been all this time. Mr Pratt, could you drive this second muddy-wheeled truck forward a few metres, so it can be opened up at the back.'

'Right then,' said Mr Pratt.

He climbed up into the cabin. The engine started up with a jolting roar and the truck rolled ahead of the rest of the line of vehicles. It moved slowly through ninety degrees and stopped with a sharp hiss of hydraulic brakes. Mr Pratt hopped down, and unbolted the rear of the truck. As the bolt clanged back and the truck's rear end swung open, we could see that the inside was filled with hundreds of cardboard boxes. One or two of them had been opened. Copies of *March of the Zombies 3* were clearly visible.

'Wow, that was risky, wasn't it?' cried Luke. 'Leaving all those discs right here? Anyone could have found them!'

'Not really,' I said. 'Yesterday, during our visit, Stephen Dale told us himself that he's the only person who controls all the movements of vehicles around here.

All he had to do was make sure this particular truck wasn't used. Then the discs could be hidden here, right under everyone's noses.'

The two police officers advanced on Len and Stephen Dale.

'I've never seen those before!' cried Len, pointing to the truck.

'Dad, forget it,' said Stephen in a low voice. 'We're finished.'

The pair of them looked tired and unhappy, like leftover sandwiches after a birthday party. Remember how, back at the start of Chapter One, I said this case got me thinking about motives? Len Dale came over to me, and said something which made me feel like a leftover sandwich too.

'You're right about what we did, young man,' he said. 'But not about why we did it. Yes, this company is in deep financial trouble. Yes, we needed cash, and we needed it fast. But not for ourselves. Without the money from selling those discs, we won't be able to pay our staff this month. Dozens of people work here, they rely on us, and I'm proud of them. Stephen and I have put years and years of hard work into this place and we were *determined* to stop it all being ruined because of a few bad debts. We didn't want to sell up, or close the depot, it would be like spitting in the faces of every worker here.

132

So we took a risk and it didn't pay off. I know, we treated Peter Lyndon appallingly, and I'm sorry. But as we saw it, it was injustice for one person weighed against injustice for dozens of people. What would you have done, young man? Still, you found us out and that's the important thing, eh? Got any bright ideas about how we can save everyone's jobs now?'

He gave me a weary smile. As the police officers led him and his son away, I felt a cold, liquid sensation of misery creep through me. 'What would you have done, young man?' The words kept zinging around my brain like a rubber ball in a lift.

'Well done, Saxby,' said Luke, beaming. 'Danielle was right: you're a genius.'

'You've got our friend Peter Lyndon out of a lot of trouble, there,' said Mr Pratt. 'Congratulations, lad.'

Peter Lyndon, looking thoroughly worn out, shook my hand. 'Thank you,' he said softly. He swiped at his eyes, which were going a bit watery and then he walked away.

I returned to my shed and flopped into my Thinking Chair. It had started raining again. I sat there for a while, pen poised over my notebook, lost in thought.

Did Len and Stephen deserve any sympathy? Can doing a good thing for lots of people ever be justified, if it means that one person suffers as a result? Is it ever right to do something bad for a good reason?

I couldn't make up my mind. What do *you* think?

A few days later, I heard that an enormous pile of waiting-to-be-mailed games that Stephen Dale had packaged up were found at Dales in a toilet marked *Out of Order*. *I guess there's some small measure of honesty in his and Len's web of deceit,* I thought to myself, *otherwise they wouldn't have bothered mailing out anything at all!*

A few days after that, I heard that Buy-Big-Bargains had shut down the auction and that the Dales had been charged with fraud, although they had refunded all the money that had been sent to them online. The workers at Dales Ltd had clubbed together and put their own money into the company, to keep it going until things improved. Which was something I really —

Plip, plip.

What was that? I looked up at the ceiling of my shed to see drips of rain squeezing out around the sides of my repair! Argghhhh!

I phoned Muddy. He hurried over. He took one look at my handiwork. 'Noooo, dum-dum, you put the patch on the *outside* of the roof!'

I slumped back into my Thinking Chair and groaned. Case closed.

CASE FILE EIGHTEEN:

THE
SHATTERED
BOX

CHAPTER
ONE

ONCE I SOLVED A CASE I called *The Mystery of the Sleeping Cactus* by spending four days watching people go in and out of a shoe shop. And there was a six week period during which I took daily measurements of the shadows cast by the trees on the St Egbert's School sports field. They were a vital clue in *The Adventure of the Martian Cyclist*.

Both these cases were far too routine and easy-to-crack to be worth telling you about here. I only mention them at all because they're examples of how detective work is all about slowly and carefully sifting through the evidence. Running about and getting into dangerous situations happens a lot less than you might think.

The case of *The Shattered Box* is an interesting one, because it's another example of the slow-and-careful approach. It was quite a small mystery, which was cleared up in the space of a single school day. However, it involved a problem which, at first sight, seemed totally baffling. Slightly crazy, even.

It all took place on the first day back at school after half-term. Everyone feels a bit miserable on the first day back, especially the teachers, but I was feeling extra glum. I still hadn't sorted out the leak in the roof of my garden shed – or Crime HQ as I prefer to call it. I'd had to shift my filing cabinet of case notes out of the way of the drips. I was now waiting for my friend George 'Muddy' Whitehouse (that scruffy but brilliant Guru of Gadgets) to find time to come over and fix it.

'How about tonight?' I suggested, as we trudged past the school gates. I had to raise my voice because there was a strong wind whistling around the school's car park.

'Can't tonight,' said Muddy, his tatty school bag slung over his shoulder. 'Promised my friend from next door I'd put extra-grip wheels on his bike.'

'Tomorrow?'

'I'm fixing Mrs Penzler's MP3 player tomorrow.'

I grumbled under my breath.

'I told you,' he said, 'you should have got me to do it. But oooh nooo, Saxby knows better, Saxby wants to tackle it himself. You know you're totally rubbish at stuff like that. You're at the back of the queue now, you'll just have to wait.'

I grumbled under my breath all the way across the car park. I grumbled some more as we made our way down the corridor that ran past the school office. Then I heard someone else grumbling.

It was the school secretary, Mrs McEwan. She was standing in the doorway of the office, hands on hips. She was tottering back and forth on her chunky high-heel shoes as if she was doing a dance called the I-Can't-Quite-Make-Up-My-Mind.

'Of all the days for this to happen,' she grumbled. 'Typical! Just what I do *not* need!'

'Got a problem, Mrs McEwan?' I asked.

'Yes, I most certainly have!' she cried, turning to face me. 'Good morning, Saxby. Hello, George.' She tugged a few stray wisps of hair back into place. Her smudgy lipstick and miniature skirt were so brightly coloured that they made the rest of her look pale by comparison.

I glanced past her, into the office. It was a wreck. Pieces of paper were strewn all over the floor, along with the contents of her desk's drawers and a jumble of pens and paper clips.

'I don't want to be rude, Mrs McEwan,' said Muddy, 'but this place looks worse than my room.'

'Someone has ransacked the office!' wailed Mrs McEwan.

'Why? When?' I said. I took a quick look at the wall

clock nearby. A-ha, good, there were at least fifteen minutes to go before registration. Plenty of time. 'Tell me what happened.'

Mrs McEwan let out a loud huff of frustration. 'I am *supposed* to be sticking to my new system of tidiness and efficiency! I'd been doing so well! And now *this*!'

'Did you discover it when you arrived?' I asked. 'Did it happen some time during the night?'

'Oh no,' said Mrs McEwan. 'I've been here a while. Someone did this within the last half an hour! I can only suppose they were looking for something to steal.'

'Did anyone see anything?' I said.

'No,' replied Mrs McEwan, 'but the Head heard a thump.'

'A thump?'

I jotted down some notes. The sequence of events had been as follows:

7:30 a.m. – Mrs McEwan arrives at school. Today, there's a PTA meeting in the main hall, plus some visitors are expected and there's a lot she needs to get ready.

7:31 a.m. – Mrs M goes down to staff room to make a cup of tea. Returns with tea. Office is as usual.

7:36 a.m. – Head arrives at school. Head and Mrs M chat about Saturday night's *Dance Insanity* on TV. Head makes cup of tea. Goes directly to her private office, tucked away along corridor running parallel to school office.

7:48 a.m. – Two scheduled visitors arrive: 1) Mr Gray, from the local council and 2) a man from 'Ben's Bugs', who's got a vanload of exotic insects outside which he's due to exhibit in various classrooms today. Mrs M directs both of them to the staff room to make themselves cups of tea.

7:50 a.m. – Mrs M enters main hall, close to office, to get things ready for PTA meeting.

8:16 a.m. – Head hears thump in office. Calls out 'Everything all right out there?' to Mrs M, thinking Mrs M has returned and has maybe dropped something. No reply.

8:17 a.m. – Head comes out to investigate. Office is total mess! Goes to main hall, fetches Mrs M. Both return. Head tells Mrs M off for having disgustingly scruffy office. Whatever happened to new system of tidiness and efficiency? Mrs M declares that office has been ransacked! Both express horror at the state of society.

8:18 a.m. – First parents arrive for PTA (Mrs Reynolds and Mr Pollard, then Mrs Brewer a few moments later) and see office. All express horror at the state of society. Head tells Mrs M to get this business sorted out as Mr Gray from the council will take a dim view of school's standards if he sees the mess. Head leads parents into main hall.

8:22 a.m. – S Smart and G Whitehouse arrive.

'I don't know where to start,' wailed Mrs McEwan, gazing sadly across the thick scattering of litter on the office floor. 'Thank goodness this didn't happen a few weeks ago.'

'Why's that?' I said.

'Because there would have been twice the mess then,' she said. 'Between you and me, I've been letting the place get a bit messy. The Head's been complaining. That's why I worked out my new system of tidiness and efficiency. Every last piece of paper and item of stationery logged and listed on the computer, clutter reduced to a minimum, paperwork organised into neat piles. I even chucked out my lucky biro, the broken one.'

'So the Head's been much happier recently?' suggested Muddy.

'No, she can't understand how I organise my new system of tidiness and efficiency. She says it's illogical. Never mind, I know where everything is, and that's the important thing. I've cut down the amount of paper in here by more than half!'

That was quite hard to believe, looking at the mess. Mrs McEwan, Muddy and I tiptoed around it all as much as we could, our feet crunching against things now and again.

The office had changed quite a lot since I'd last been in there. Everything was sorted into neat little trays, or would have been if it wasn't all over the floor. Even the chunky paper shredder had been replaced with a simple slot poised above the (currently empty) paper-recycling box.

'Looks like they left the computer alone,' muttered Mrs McEwan. 'That doesn't appear to have been touched at all.'

Something caught my eye, sitting on top of a heap of scattered papers, next to Mrs McEwan's star-footed swivel chair. I stepped around the paper heap and, crouching down, I nudged the object over on to its side.

It was a large metal cash box, one of those round-cornered boxes for keeping money or other valuables in. Its lid was slightly bent, and swung loosely open. Its hefty lock had been smashed apart. A small pile of coins had fallen out of it.

I looked up at Mrs McEwan. 'Have they taken much cash?'

'None, by the look of it,' said Mrs McEwan. 'There was only some loose change in there anyway.'

'That's odd,' I muttered. 'Where was the box sitting?'

'Right there on the desk,' said Mrs McEwan. 'It wasn't hidden away. Why would they smash it open and then steal nothing from it?'

'Perhaps,' said Muddy, 'they expected to find it full of cash? They wouldn't know those coins were all that was in it until they'd opened it, would they?'

143

'They weren't after money,' I mumbled, picking up the shattered box and turning it over in my hands. 'Breaking this thing open was just an afterthought.'

'How could you possibly know that?' asked Mrs McEwan.

There were a couple of simple observations about the box which indicated that the thieves hadn't been interested in stealing money. Can you spot them?

'The cash box was sitting in plain sight, right there on the desk,' I said. 'If all they'd wanted was money, they'd have broken it open straight away. But they didn't. They ransacked the rest of the office first.'

'How can you tell?' said Muddy.

'Because the box is on top of this heap of paper,' I said. 'The paper was dropped first, the box opened afterwards.'

Tapping the box's ruined lock with one finger, I started looking around for . . .

'Look!' I said. 'There's a mark on the edge of the desk, a little chunk's been taken out of it. Was this here before?'

'No,' said Mrs McEwan. 'I see what you're getting at. They bashed the box on the desk to force it open.'

'That must have been the thump that the Head heard!' cried Muddy.

'Exactly,' I said. 'When the Head called out, the thieves realised someone was close by and made a run for it. By the time the Head came out of her office, they were long gone.'

'Even if they didn't want money,' said Muddy, 'they must have been after *something*. What's missing?'

Mrs McEwan snorted crossly at the mess for a few moments. 'Well, I had a new box of elastic bands on the desk, I can't see that anywhere, and the two pencils from my pen pot have gone, but apart from that . . . Well, it's anyone's guess. All that's in here is ordinary school paperwork, nothing valuable or secret, no information you couldn't get elsewhere or that you couldn't be told about, if you asked nicely.'

'So,' I said, 'someone wrecks the office, smashes the cash box, and runs off with a handful of stationery.'

'As a robbery, it's slightly crazy,' commented Muddy.

A Page From My Notebook

Where on earth do I start? This incident has some very strange features. As Muddy said, the thieves wanted SOMETHING. From the look of the office, they were SEARCHING. But for what?

Thought No. 1: Could we be making a mistake here? Could the mess be accounted for by a freak gust of wind or a stray cat going a bit loopy? I don't think so. How do you explain the shattered box, for a start?

Thought No. 2: That box is a vital clue. It must have taken a LOT of force to smash it. Whatever the thieves were looking for, they wanted it REALLY badly! The deduction that their search was FRANTIC is backed up by two things: 1) The way all those papers were scattered about and 2) The way the thieves risked discovery – they

– struck at the start of an ordinary school day, ANYONE might have spotted them!

Thought No. 3: The thieves aren't outsiders. A burglar would have nicked the cash box and the computer. The office was searched for something specific, therefore the culprits KNEW it would be there, therefore they're almost certainly connected with the school.

Follow-up question: Clearly, they weren't just after a box of elastic bands and two pencils. So why take them at all?

Follow-up question, part B: If my Thought No. 3 is correct, could the thieves still be here in school? Or did they take what they wanted and run?

My plan of action:

1. Mrs M said that everything in the office is logged on the computer. So I must work out EXACTLY what's been stolen – I can't discover WHY the incident happened until I know WHAT the thieves were after.

2. Must question those three parents who arrived for PTA meeting at 8:18 a.m. Did they see anyone leaving the school? Or walking away from the direction of the office?

3. This is going to take time – must ask Mrs Penzler if I can skip PE this morning. (Note to self: Before asking, practise using lost-puppy-dog-oh-please-please-please expression!)

CHAPTER
TWO

OUR FORM TEACHER, MRS PENZLER, can be a bit on the stern side. Nothing cracks her tough, concrete-like shell. I've seen kids turn on the tears and pretend to be suffering from terrible diseases and swear to her – on the lives of their beloved mothers – that their homework was eaten by a donkey. Nothing. Zilch. Nada.

So I was pleasantly surprised when she let me off PE. I didn't even need to use my lost-puppy-dog-oh-please-please-please expression. Thinking about it, it was probably because she'd had first-hand experience of what a brilliant schoolboy detective I am. Or possibly because Mrs McEwan is her best buddy.

'You can investigate for an hour, Saxby,' she barked, 'then I want you back in class. We've got the man from

Ben's Bugs here today to show us his exotic insects.'

I quickly returned to the office. By now, Mrs McEwan had scooped up all the scattered papers and had dumped them in a big heap on her desk.

'I'll go through them in a minute,' I said. 'Has the PTA meeting started yet?'

'No,' said Mrs McEwan, glancing up at the clock, 'you've got a few minutes.'

'Don't those things usually happen out of school hours?' I muttered, sifting through the top of the paper pile.

'Usually. But this is an important one, about the curriculum. It has to be held this week and now is the only time everyone could make it. It's likely to go on for hours.'

At that moment, the blood froze in my veins. Not at the thought of the PTA meeting (although that does often happen to teachers, apparently), but as I watched two people walking past the office.

One of them was the Head. It wasn't her who froze my blood (although that also often happens to teachers, apparently), it was the man walking along beside her.

He was stooping and round-shouldered, with thinning hair slicked across his flattened skull. His face looked like it had been designed by a mad scientist, and from the sleeves of his dark jacket hung meaty, sallow-skinned hands. As he and the Head passed by, he flicked a look in my direction. It was then that my blood froze.

'That's Mr Gray, from the local council,' whispered Mrs McEwan. 'He's here for the PTA meeting too. Something to do with inspecting standards of something-or-other. Horrible man, always rude, the poor Head can't stand him. He's been here a few times.'

'I see,' I said, trying not to sound scared. 'I'll be back soon, I'm going to ask a few questions.'

Notebook in hand, I went into the assembly hall. About fifteen or twenty adults were milling about in little groups, sipping their tea and waiting for the PTA meeting to begin.

I soon found the three parents who had arrived at 8.18 a.m. – Mrs Reynolds, Mr Pollard and Mrs Brewer. I asked all three if they'd seen anyone – anyone at all – coming from the direction of the office at around 8:17 a.m., just after the Head heard the thump. They hadn't. They expressed horror at the state of society, I thanked them politely, and I moved on.

Mr Gray was on the other side of the hall, terrifying some parents by standing there and talking to them. Seeing him there jogged my memory about something else which I'd put down in my notebook. Or rather, seeing him there turned my blood to water and *then* jogged my memory.

I went over to a couple of teachers, Mr Nailshott and Mrs Womsey. I asked them if they were in the staff room this morning, between about 7.45 a.m. and 8.20 a.m.

Answer: yes. They went back and forth between the staff room and their classrooms, but yes, between them, they were there during that whole period. So were many other members of staff.

I asked them if today's two visitors – Mr Gray from the council and the man from Ben's Bugs – were in the staff room too.

Answer: no. Mr Gray had appeared very briefly, then hurried out clutching the seat of his trousers. They hadn't seen the bug man at all.

'The man with the bugs is due to visit my class at eleven,' said Mrs Womsey. 'I hope he's not got lost somewhere.'

'Mr Gray left clutching his trousers?' I asked, puzzled.

'Yes, like that,' said Mr Nailshott, pointing across the room. Mr Gray was scuttling away, walking as if he had an elephant trying to escape from his underpants.

The teachers asked me if I was investigating . . . [*shh, whisper, whisper*] . . . this Morning's Incident. I said I was. They expressed horror at the state of society. I thanked them politely and returned to Mrs McEwan. The previously-scattered office paperwork was still perched in a large wobbly pile on her desk.

'Got any suspects yet?' asked Mrs McEwan.

'What, apart from the entire school including every pupil and all the members of staff?' I replied. 'No, not really. However, I have just discovered something highly suspicious. Our two visitors this morning, did you actually show them to the staff room?'

'No, I just gave them directions and off they went. I would have taken them down there normally, but I was so busy with the PTA meeting. Why?'

'Both Mr Gray *and* this bug guy are unaccounted for at the time of the robbery. Er, incident. Whatever. Neither of them was in the staff room, as they were supposed to be.'

Mrs McEwan let out a little gasp. 'You're right,' she breathed, her eyes staring alarmingly, 'that *is* highly suspicious.'

But was it? Either of these people *could* have done it, but neither of them fitted in with Thought No. 3 in my notes (see the end of Chapter One). Or was there something about them I didn't know yet? Did Mr Gray really have elephantpants-itis? Or was it a bluff, so that he could go sneaking around the school? And what had happened to the bug guy? Where *was* he?

The obvious thing to do was to question the pair of them. But I didn't fancy exchanging so much as a word with that Mr Gray. I was scared my bones might turn to dust and I'd slump to the floor in a jellyish flop of arms and legs! And the bug guy didn't seem to be around anywhere. Where was he?

I'd kept putting it to the back of my mind, trying not to even consider it, but there was a disturbing fact I had to face: almost *anyone* in the school *could* have wrecked the office. It was done at the start of a normal school day, and *hundreds* of kids and adults were around. My suspect list was longer than the lunch queue!

'Look, I don't want to hurry you, luvvy,' said Mrs McEwan, 'but if you're going through all this paperwork for clues, I need you to do it now. I've got a lot of work to do.'

'Oh, yeah, sorry, right,' I said.

I opened my notebook and reminded myself about point one in my Plan of Action. The first (actually, the *only*) thing to do now was to work out *why* the office had been wrecked and what had been taken (apart from the box of elastic bands and the two pencils). In amongst this whopping great heap of paperwork was the clue I needed!

Thanks to her new system of tidiness and efficiency, Mrs McEwan could print out a complete log of office items for me, so that I could compare it with what was still actually here in the office. She assured me that her list was complete and accurate. (It didn't include things like furniture or the phone, obviously – we'd have noticed if any of that had gone!)

I won't copy out the full list here. It would make very boring reading and it would take up the whole of the rest of this book! It broke down roughly as follows:

• Letters about various things, to give to pupils, to give to parents.

• Letters about various things, returned from parents.

• Other letters and everyday correspondence.

• Items of stationery – paper, printer ink cartridges, pens, paper clips, etc, etc.

• Other items – cash box [now broken], paper shredder, educational reference books, etc, etc.

• Reports *by* the school – about pupils' grades, etc.

• Reports *to* the school – from the council, from the government, etc.

• Mrs McEwan's stuff from home – tea mug, etc.

All pretty standard stuff. I then went through the pile of paperwork on Mrs McEwan's desk, scribbling into my notebook as I went, sorting things out into piles as best I could. Soon, I had a complete list of everything.

Nervously, I picked my way, bit by bit, through the two lists. I compared them line by line. The minutes were ticking away. Soon, I'd have to be back in class.

With a couple of minutes to spare, I finished the job. I made another note in my notebook.

'Well?' asked Mrs McEwan expectantly.

'I've now worked out *exactly* what's been taken,' I said. 'Apart from the box of elastic bands and the two pencils, I mean.'

'What, then?' gasped Mrs McEwan. 'What were they searching for? What did they steal?'

CHAPTER
THREE

MRS MCEWAN STARED AT ME for a moment. 'You're joking,' she said.

'Do I look like I'm joking?' I said, as flat-faced and un-jokey as I could possibly be. 'Nothing has gone. Nothing. Every last letter, report, file, paper clip and piece of paper is still here. Apart from the box of elastic bands and the two pencils.'

Mrs McEwan put her hands to the side of her head and pulled a face which looked like someone trying to lay an egg. 'So . . . it wasn't even a robbery? It wasn't thieves? Nobody was out to find *anything*?' She shook her head sharply and flapped her hands. 'No, no, correction. This *was* all about stealing a box of elastic bands and two pencils!' She slumped on to her swivel chair. 'Oh, I don't know what to think.'

'There's something I'm missing here,' I muttered to myself.

'Perhaps someone was just out to cause trouble?' said Mrs McEwan. 'Simple as that. You know, nick a few elastic bands, make a mess for someone else to clear up, and giggle about it behind the bike shed later on.'

'I don't think so,' I said. 'The presence of the shattered box indicates that they were definitely after something.'

'But *what*?' cried Mrs McEwan. 'If nothing's gone, there was nothing here that they wanted.'

Suddenly, an explanation smacked me on the head like a pencil fired from an elastic band. Adding what Mrs McEwan had just said to the fact that the culprits almost certainly *were* after something specific, there was a conclusion to be made!

Can you spot it?

Of course! Why hadn't I seen it before? *That* was the vital thing I'd been overlooking!

'They *were* searching the office,' I said. 'But nothing has gone. Which means that they *didn't find* what they were looking for. Whatever they were after is *still here.*'

At that moment, the bell for the next lesson sounded. Time for me to return to class. I almost squeaked with frustration!

The object, the target, the whatever-it-was they were looking for, it was in amongst the paperwork here in front of me. Think think think! Was there anything unusual I'd seen, anything even slightly out of the ordinary that might give me some sort of a lead?

'C'mon, off you go,' said Mrs McEwan. 'Mrs Penzler's not impressed by lateness, you know that.'

Think!

There were three possibilities. As I'd gone through that pile of paper, there had been three items – three printed letters – with features which were slightly out of the ordinary. (And I do mean 'slightly'! They might have had *no* connection to the case *at all*. I was clutching at straws here, trying to find a clue.) These letters were:

1. A permission letter for Sinead Crane in Mrs Womsey's class, filled in by her mum and covering a class trip to Pizza Panik (to have a go at making them, not to eat them!). Unusual feature: the letter had clearly been screwed up and binned – it was extremely crumpled and had what looked like food stains on it.

2. A letter to the Head from Donald Pollard, dad of Paul Pollard (also in Mrs Womsey's class), complaining about the quality of school dinners. Unusual feature: it was really very, very critical indeed. It was so harsh it almost made me want to hug a dinner lady in sympathy. Almost.

3. Another permission letter, this time for Katie Brewer in my class, filled in by her mum and covering a forthcoming trip to the local theatre. Unusual feature: as well as Katie's mum's signature on the front, there was a second signature (someone called Ellie Brewer) written half a dozen times on the back.

'Just borrowing these!' I cried, grabbing them and scooting out of the office. 'Important clues! I'll bring them back later!'

I hurried away before Mrs McEwan could object. When I arrived at my classroom, a man wearing a bright green stripey shirt and a pair of round green-framed glasses was standing in front of the class, arranging see-through plastic boxes on Mrs Penzler's desk.

Oh, at last! *This* was the guy from Ben's Bugs. I scooted over to my seat and paid attention, as Mrs Penzler gave me a just-in-time-young-man look.

'Hello everyone,' said the Bug Man in a voice as lively

and interesting as cold porridge. 'My name's Ben. I'm from Ben's Bugs. We do roadshows and visit places, showing people our collections of exotic insects.'

Limply, he cast a hand across the plastic boxes. We all strained to see inside them. They seemed to be mostly filled with twigs and leaves.

All the time, Bug Man's eyes kept scanning the floor, and the area under our desks, and the area under Mrs Penzler.

'Today I've got some interesting specimens for you to have a look at, including . . . er, umm, well, I was going to show you the Red-Backed Pinching Beetle of Western Sumatra, which likes to hide and then spring out on its prey but, er, umm . . . Must have left it behind . . . I hope . . . Since there's a loose lid on one of these, umm, er . . . Gives you a very nasty bite, it does . . . Anyway, here's an interesting specimen, it's a cute little caterpillar . . .'

To cut a long lesson short, I hadn't realised it was possible to make creepy crawlies seem quite so boring. Even the really vicious ones which eat each other became dull and ordinary when described in Bug Man's droning voice. The whole class gazed sleepily at fascinating examples of the Tiny Blue Butterfly of Northern Greenland and the Four-Legged Ant of Mongolia . . . yawn . . . zzzzzzz . . .

'Any questions?' he said about five years later.

Two or three hands went up, including mine. Bug Man pointed at me. 'Yes?'

'Can I ask you where you were at exactly eight-eighteen this morning?'

Mrs Penzler glared at me. 'Insect-related questions please, Saxby.'

'Oh, right,' I said. 'OK, have you lost one of your bugs? Earlier on, you seemed to have lost something?'

'No,' said Bug Man, decisively, going slightly red in the face. 'No, no, not at all, no. That would be very bad of me. No, definitely not. Next question?'

The bell sounded for break about ten minutes later. Mrs Penzler, smiling, thanked the Bug Man very, very much for such a fascinating talk. She seemed to have loved every minute of it. The whole class gazed sleepily at a fascinating example of the Weird Teacher of St Egbert's.

I hurried outside, clutching the three letters I'd borrowed from the office. I had about fifteen minutes to find whatever background information these letters could provide.

Luckily, Muddy came over to me for a chat. So I sent him looking for the kids I wanted to talk to. I sat on one of the wooden benches beneath the line of trees that bordered the sports field. Nearby was the window of the staff room, which was filled all break with a shifting mass of teachers and parents – the PTA meeting must have been taking time out along with the rest of us. The only fixed point was (shudder) Mr Gray, who was sitting in there glaring out at the world until the bell went again.

Anyway, with Muddy's help I managed to hold three short conversations before the next lesson. Here's what was said (I've not bothered with any of the 'hello', 'goodbye' or 'isn't it shocking what's happened in the office' bits):

Short Conversation No. 1 – Sinead Crane

S Smart: Why was your permission letter here crumpled up and thrown away?

S Crane: Well, my mum filled it in and then she changed her mind and said I couldn't go within a mile of Pizza Panik.

S Smart: Why?

S Crane (deep sigh): She's a health inspector. After she signed the letter three weeks ago she did a surprise inspection of Pizza Panik's kitchens. And she says they were filthy. She threw the letter in the bin.

S Smart: And you got it back out again?

S Crane (pauses): Yes. It's not fair! I want to go on that trip! She said herself that Pizza Panik will have to clean up now, or the council will close them down! It's not fair!

S Smart: So your mum works for the council? Does she know this Mr Gray who's here today?

S Crane: Eurgh, yes. Horrible man. Apparently, he goes through people's desks when they're out, counts up their paper clips, then tries to get them sacked for nicking official council stationery. He's tried that one on Mum twice.

S Smart: Hmm, nice guy.

Short Conversation No. 2 – Katie Brewer

S Smart: On the back of your permission letter, someone else has signed it too, as well as your mum, someone called Ellie Brewer?

K Brewer (looking at the letter): Oh, that's my great-aunt, my dad's aunt. Things were a bit difficult at home in the weeks before half-term. The poor lady was getting confused, I saw she'd signed the newspaper several times too. Mum's been very upset.

S Smart: Upset? Aunt Ellie's been ill?

K Brewer: She died exactly two weeks ago. She'd been ill for ages.

S Smart: Oh! I'm sorry, I didn't mean to —

K Brewer: It's OK, I hardly knew her. I only met her when she came to live with us a few weeks ago. But she and Mum were close – Mum said she didn't want Aunt Ellie to go into a hospice. So she came to us.

S Smart: I'm so sorry. No wonder your mum's been upset.

K Brewer: She was very distracted and in a funny mood all last week, during half-term, but I think she's feeling better now. She's on the PTA, she's at the meeting today.

S Smart: Yes, I asked her a couple of questions this morning.

Short Conversation No. 3 – Paul Pollard

S Smart: Why did your dad write to the Head about the school dinners? I mean, I see his point, but . . .

P Pollard: I d'no. They're rubbish.

S Smart: Was there a particular dinner that enraged him? An ingredient? A menu?

P Pollard: D'no.

S Smart: Has he spoken to you about why he was so angry? Is he still angry about it?

P Pollard: No. D'no.

S Smart: How did the Head react? Has she replied to his letter yet?

P Pollard: D'no.

S Smart: Perhaps I should have asked your dad all this when I spoke to him earlier?

P Pollard: Yeah, s'pose.

The bell sounded and everyone slouched back indoors. As I was bumped along back to class in the river of pupils, several possibilities occurred to me.

Things were becoming a little clearer. But not for a moment did I suspect what would happen next!

A Page From My Notebook

Some possible scenarios, based on my three short conversations:

1. COULD Sinead Crane, having rescued that permission letter from the bin, now be having second thoughts? Could it be that she realises she'll be in trouble if her mum finds out she's going on the Pizza Panik trip? Could she be trying to get that permission letter back?

2. COULD Mr Gray be up to some sort of trick? Could he be trying to make St Egbert's look bad? If so, why?

3. COULD Paul Pollard's dad, who's on the PTA, have changed his mind about that letter of complaint? Could it be that he wants to find it and remove it from the office, so that people like Mr Gray don't find it and start causing a fuss?

WAIT! SUDDEN THOUGHT!

4. COULD . . . the HEAD have done it? Could SHE be the one who wants to remove Mr Pollard's complaint letter from the office? Could it be that she was LYING about hearing that thump this morning?

IMPORTANT!!! MUST NOT forget that these three letters might have NOTHING TO DO with the case! I only picked them out because they were the only things with unusual features. But I'm still guessing. Nothing can be confirmed.

However . . .

If the Head *is* involved . . .

What do I do now?

CHAPTER
FOUR

MRS MCEWAN FLAGGED ME DOWN as I passed the office on my way back to class.

'Saxby,' she hissed. 'Come in here! Look at this!'

The office was absolutely spotless. Not a single sheet of paper in sight.

'Wow, that's *tidy*!' I cried. 'Well done.'

'Noooo,' she wailed. 'This morning's raider has struck again during break! Now *all* that paperwork has been stolen! The whole lot! I went to the staff room for a cup of tea —'

('Er, exactly how many times a day do you go to the staff room for a cup of tea, Mrs McEwan?' I wanted to ask.)

'— and when I got back, that pile on my desk was gone! I was only away for ten minutes! This is a disaster!'

'No,' I said, 'it's proof that I was right. Remember, I said that whoever-it-was hadn't found what they were looking for? Well, this proves it. They had to come back. It was break, there were people about, they might only have had a few seconds alone. So they had no time to search again, instead they took it all away.'

'But why?' gasped Mrs McEwan.

'Well, to search through it somewhere else,' I said. 'Somewhere out of sight.'

'What am I supposed to do now?' grumbled Mrs McEwan. 'They've run off with all my work.'

'If I were you,' I said, 'I'd have a discreet look around in cupboards and under chairs. This whoever-it-is will want to search that paperwork, take whatever-it-is they want and then get rid of the rest of it. Fast. There's too much of it to just put in a waste-paper basket, and I doubt they'd want to risk taking it all out to the big recycling bin because they'd probably be seen. My guess is they'll dump it all somewhere.'

Mrs McEwan snorted unhappily as she whipped a lipstick out of her handbag and re-smeared her lips.

'In the meantime,' I said, 'I've got to get back to class again.'

I couldn't concentrate during maths. Well, to be honest, my concentration during maths is usually pretty feeble, but today I really definitely couldn't concentrate.

I looked again at the last entries in my notebook (from the end of Chapter Three). This latest development took *two* people off my list of suspects. Two of the people I'd mentioned in those notes definitely didn't do that breaktime raid on the office.

Can you name them?

The first one I could eliminate was Mr Gray. I'd seen him sitting in the staff room all the way through break. So he'd had no opportunity to go to the office.

The second person was Sinead. I was with her for the first part of break. She *could* have raided the office afterwards, but she'd have to have been *very* quick about it. In any case, if she was after that crumpled-up permission letter, she knew I had it with me. There'd be no point in her raiding the office!

Once again, the Bug Man was left unaccounted for. Where had he been during break? Was that stuff about a lost beetle just a smokescreen? But . . . did he deserve to be on my suspect list in the first place? I still couldn't see what motive he could have. I still couldn't make a connection between him and the office paperwork, or with the school in general.

Ideas and theories swirled around my brain, taking up the space where maths should have been. Luckily, Mrs Penzler didn't ask me anything, otherwise I'd probably have just blurble-blurbled some rubbish or other.

The moment lunchtime began, I hurried back to the office. To my delight – and amazement – the stolen heap of paperwork was back on Mrs McEwan's desk.

'You found it!' I exclaimed.

Mrs McEwan nodded. 'You were right. It was all

sitting in one of the cubicles in the ladies' toilets. Just over there, next to the main hall.'

The *ladies'* toilets? Did that mean I could eliminate any male suspects from my list? Was the Bug Man now in the clear? Was Paul Pollard's dad out of the picture?

'And guess what I found sitting on top of the pile?' said Mrs McEwan.

'What?'

She held up an unopened box of elastic bands and a pair of pencils.

'Interesting,' I said. 'They put back the things they took. Did they have a sudden attack of guilt?'

I gazed grimly at the heap of paperwork. 'Er, y'know,' I said, 'the next thing to do is to see if anything's been taken from amongst this pile.'

'I thought you did that earlier?' said Mrs McEwan.

'I did, but it's all been taken and brought back since then, hasn't it? I'm going to have to check the whole lot a second time.'

I groaned. Loudly.

CHAPTER
FIVE

ONCE MY *SECOND* CROSS-CHECK OF the entire office was complete, I sat back on the swivel chair. I swivelled a little.

'Well?' said Mrs McEwan. 'Nothing was missing last time. What's gone from the pile now that the culprit has had a chance to search it again?'

'Nothing,' I said. 'Once again, nothing at all.'

'Oh, come *on!*' cried Mrs McEwan. 'They took all this stuff away. Their first search had to be at lightning speed, but this time they could have been as slow and careful as they liked. And they *still* took nothing? This puts us back to square one, doesn't it?'

'No,' I said, grinning. 'This is exactly the result I was hoping for. If they've taken nothing from the office paperwork second time around, it's a big help to my investigation. It confirms something.'

'Huh?' said Mrs McEwan, screwing up her nose. 'How?'

This case was rapidly being narrowed down! One aspect of the mystery could now be clarified!

Have you worked it out?

'This confirms something very important,' I said. 'If they took nothing this second time, it means that, once again, they didn't find what they were looking for.'

'Yes, so?' said Mrs McEwan.

'So why would that be? Because what they were looking for *wasn't there*. And the only pieces of the office paperwork which weren't there were these three letters that I took away with me at break. It *must* be one of those letters they're after!'

Mrs McEwan nodded, her eyes shut in a why-didn't-I-think-of-that expression. 'Yes, this clears up the whole problem of what it is they wanted in the first place. Up to now, we've been guessing.'

'Right,' I said. 'I only picked out these letters because they were the only ones with anything unusual about them. They might have been totally unconnected to all this. But now, I can say for sure that one of them *is* the vital clue.'

My re-sorting of the paperwork had turned the one big heap into a series of much smaller heaps. As I spoke, Mrs McEwan started re-re-sorting everything, to put things back into line with her new, personal system of tidiness and efficiency.

'Let's see . . .' she muttered to herself, 'I need the figures on . . . yes, that can go there, and these need to be put in here . . . [*shuffle, shuffle*] Now, where's the last

SATS report . . . [*shuffle*] must be here . . . [*shuffle*] somewhere . . . [*shuffle*] . . . *Wait!* It's *gone*! Saxby, the SATS report's *gone*! They've *taken* it! *That's* what they were after! It's totally *gone*! What are we —'

She suddenly halted in mid-panic. 'Oh. It's right here in front of me. Sorry. What am I like? Right under my nose all the time! *This* is why I need my new system of tidiness and efficiency.'

Mrs McEwan's panic had distracted me. I was suddenly reminded of a famous detective story I'd read at home, *The Purloined Letter* by a guy called Edgar Allan Poe. In the story, nobody can find a stolen letter because they're searching in all the sneaky, hidden places, when all the time it's sitting right in front of —

Wait a minute.

A thought snapped into my head: I wonder if that was why —

'*Arggghh!*'

A howling cry came from outside the office. Mrs McEwan and I raced out into the corridor.

We were just in time to see the door of the men's toilets slam back on its hinges. Mr Gray leaped out, his face distorted with more emotions than I could count. His trousers were flapping around his knees and he was clutching his backside as he half-hopped, half-ran towards the car park exit.

'ARGH! ARGH! Something's bitten me! Oh my God! *Argh!* Do something, you idiots! As if I haven't got enough bottom trouble today! Oh *oww! Owwwwwww!'*

The noise quickly brought people scurrying out of the main hall and elsewhere. Everyone over the age of about twelve looked shocked and concerned. Everyone under the age of about twelve burst out laughing.

The Bug Man appeared, scooting after Mr Gray with a plastic box in his outstretched hands. 'Oi! Don't hurt it! That's a Red-Backed Pinching Beetle of Western Sumatra, it's very rare! Oi!'

The Head bustled out of the main hall and scooted after the pair of them. 'Nothing to see, everyone!' she called over her shoulder. 'Carry on as normal!'

While everyone else was either giggling loudly or else whispering that society must be in an even worse state than they'd previously feared, I wandered back into the office. My thoughts were crashing into each other like particles in a giant collider.

I took the three letters out of my pocket. I re-examined them: two permission letters – one for a visit to Pizza Panik, one for a theatre trip – and a letter of complaint about school dinners. One or other of them was the key to this mystery.

If the Bug Man *had* spent half the day looking for that missing beetle, could I remove him from the suspect list too? What did that leave me with? How did this connect to one of the letters? Was there one small piece of the jigsaw still missing?

I turned those letters over and over in my hands. *What* was I missing? Was the solution staring me in the face?

'Saxby?'

'Huh?' I said, jolted away from my reeling thoughts for a moment.

'I said, do you know the date?' said Mrs McEwan. She was back at her desk, filling out an 'Injuries on School Premises' report sheet.

Was it the seventeenth? I wasn't sure, and without Mrs McEwan switching the computer on, there wasn't an immediate way to check. I looked at the three letters I was holding. The one on top was the one about the theatre trip.

'When did this one go out?' I said. 'It's dated the fourth.'

'Er . . . the Wednesday before half-term, so that's twelve days ago.'

'Ah! So it's the sixteenth today,' I declared.

'Thanks,' said Mrs McEwan. 'Hmm,' she muttered to herself. 'What do I put for "Location of Injury"?'

'Toilets?' I suggested.

At that moment, the last piece of the puzzle fell into place. 'That's it!' I cried. 'I've got the key to the whole problem!'

'What, "toilets"?' asked Mrs McEwan.

'No,' I cried. 'The date!'

There was one little detail that didn't match up. One little detail that showed me which of the three letters was the important one, and what today's strange events had all been about.

It was a question of dates and the order in which things had happened. I thought back to those three conversations I'd had at break. Have you spotted the mismatch?

CHAPTER
SIX

AT THE END OF THE school day, five people were gathered together in the school office: me, Mrs McEwan, Mrs Penzler, Katie Brewer and Katie's mum.

'What's this about?' said Mrs Brewer. 'Will this take long? I've got shopping to do.'

'Oh, it'll only take a minute,' I said. 'I just wanted to check something.' I pulled out Katie's permission letter, the one about the theatre trip, the one with the name Ellie Brewer written half a dozen times on the back. I held it up. 'Is this what you've been looking for all day?'

Mrs Brewer smiled. 'I'm sorry, I don't know what you mean.'

'Are you sure of your facts, Saxby?' warned Mrs Penzler, eyeing me sternly. 'Mrs Brewer was in the PTA meeting until shortly after lunchtime.'

'Yes, I know,' I said. 'And yes, I'm sure. Well, er, pretty sure. I'll set out the chain of events and then you'll see what I'm talking about.'

All of them eyed me sternly now. Nervous ripples shuddered icily down the back of my neck. I was worried that what I had to say would sound ruthless and accusing and that at the very least it would upset Katie Brewer. But the truth is the truth.

'OK,' I began, my voice wobbling only slightly. 'Early this morning, Mrs Brewer arrives at school. She intends to go to the office and ask for this permission letter back. What excuse she's going to use, I don't know. But she needs this letter back at all costs.

'She gets to the office. By chance, it's empty. Mrs McEwan is busy with preparations for the PTA meeting. Mrs Brewer realises that, if she's quick, she can retrieve the letter herself. She won't even have to ask for it, which might have been awkward and suspicious in any case.

'She starts to search through the office. Mrs McEwan is now using her personal system of tidiness and efficiency. The Head can't follow the logic of this system, and neither, it turns out, can Mrs Brewer. The letter is here, right under her nose, but just like the characters in *The Purloined Letter* she can't see it for looking, if you see what I mean.

'Her search becomes frantic. Paper gets scattered everywhere. That letter has got to be here somewhere! But the seconds are ticking away, someone could walk past at any moment. As a last resort, Mrs Brewer breaks open the cash box on the desk, in case for some reason the letter is inside. It isn't.

'But the breaking of the box has been overheard. The Head calls out. Mrs Brewer realises she's on the point of being caught. She's got to get out of here. But look at this mess! In her panic, she thinks that the only thing to do is make this look like a break-in. So, flustered and not thinking straight, she simply grabs the first things she sees – a box of elastic bands and two pencils – and legs it.

'Calming down slightly, she realises that she's now going to need an alibi. Messing up the office and faking a robbery was a mistake, a moment's madness, because now questions are going to be asked. So she keeps out of sight for a few minutes. A couple of other parents arrive for the PTA. She follows along behind them and comes back to the office making it look like she's just this minute arrived at school. Oh no, shocking, look what's happened to the office!

'She goes into the hall over there, trying to decide what to do next. Can she go and ask for the letter back now? Not without looking highly suspicious. She's going to have to think of something else.

'A few minutes later, I turn up. I start asking questions about where people were at the time of the so-called robbery. Mrs Brewer realises that she's going to have to act fast, if she's going to get to the letter before I do.

'She heads back to the office at break. There's no time to search through the paperwork again, especially now it's sitting in one big heap on Mrs McEwan's desk. So, quick as she can, while everyone else from the PTA is down in the staff room, she carries the paperwork over to the ladies' loos. Out of sight, she searches through the paperwork again. But *still* she can't find that letter. What she doesn't realise is that I've already got it with me. She abandons the paperwork in the toilets. She also leaves the box of elastic bands and the two pencils. After all, she doesn't usually go around pocketing things, even if it's nothing more than elastic bands and pencils.

'By now, she sees that there are only two possibilities: either she was mistaken, and the letter was never in the office, or else I've got it. Either way, she's going to have to think carefully about what to do next. However, I've been too quick for her. I've worked out what happened, and here we are.'

'I don't understand,' said Katie. 'Why on earth would anyone be so desperate to get the letter back? It's only a simple school permission thing about a theatre trip.'

'It's not the letter,' I said. 'It's what's on the back of it. The signature of your great aunt, Ellie Brewer, written half a dozen times.'

Katie laughed. 'I told you, Aunt Ellie kept signing all sorts of funny things.'

'And perhaps that's what gave your mother the idea in the first place,' I said. 'Seeing that signature on various odds and ends.'

'Idea?' said Katie. 'Idea for what?'

'Ah, well,' I said, 'that's the one thing I don't know. I can't be sure *why* that signature is here on the back of this letter. But I do know one thing about it.'

'I've had enough of all this,' announced Mrs Brewer. 'Come on, Katie, we've got things to do. Sorry to waste your time, Mrs Penzler, Mrs McEwan.'

'Wait a moment, Mum!' cried Katie. She turned back to me. 'Saxby, what's this "one thing" you know?'

'I know that Ellie Brewer's signature on this letter is a forgery,' I said. 'Someone's been practising that signature. Probably, the forger didn't realise at first what they were writing on the back of.'

'A forged signature?' said Mrs Penzler. 'That's a very serious allegation, Saxby. How can you be sure?'

'It's a matter of dates,' I said. 'Katie told me earlier today that her great aunt died exactly two weeks ago. But this letter wasn't even printed out until the following

Wednesday. Aunt Ellie can't possibly have signed it herself.

'Katie, you also told me that your mum had been in a funny mood all last week, during half-term. You put it down to her being upset about Aunt Ellie. But it may be that she'd been trying to make sure that she got rid of any stray piece of paper she'd practised Ellie Brewer's signature on. It may be that she realised she'd written on the back of a school letter by mistake and that you'd brought that letter back here to the office. It may be that she was frantic to get the letter back. She had a PTA meeting here today, so she decided to retrieve the letter as soon as she got here.'

'But why would she want to fake that signature in the first place?' said Mrs McEwan.

'That's the part I don't know,' I said. 'I can only guess that Ellie Brewer died before signing some important document or other. But exactly what, I have no idea. The point is, this letter is proof that someone has been trying to fake Ellie Brewer's signature, for whatever reason.'

For the first time, I looked over at Mrs Brewer. She seemed oddly rigid and determined, like a last toffee that's stuck to the bottom of the tin, determined not to budge even though it knows it's going to get eaten.

'Well, you're quite a detective, Saxby, I'll give you that,' she said quietly, eyeing me.

There was silence for a moment. And then, as if the silence had suddenly punctured her confidence, Mrs Brewer dropped her gaze to the floor. She sniffed sharply. 'But as you say, you have proof. I don't suppose there's any point in denying it.'

She folded her arms. 'If you must know, it was all about her last will and testament. In the days before she died, she would pat my hand and tell me how she'd recently changed her will. She certainly had. The day after her death, I opened the will and found she'd left everything to the local cat's home.'

'So you wrote a new will?' whispered Katie, her face awash with amazement.

Mrs Brewer nodded. 'Aunt Ellie's habit of scribbling on things gave me plenty of samples of her signature. The original will gave me samples of how the witnesses to it had signed. It was easy to rewrite the thing, leaving everything to her son. Of course, if anything went wrong, any piece of paper with my practice forgeries on it would be incriminating evidence. I had to get the letter back, no matter how slim the chances that anyone would spot the mismatch of dates.'

'But luckily,' said Mrs Penzler, glancing in my direction, 'someone did spot it.'

'I've spent half my life being pleasant to that miserable old bat,' said Mrs Brewer in a low voice. 'I showed her nothing but kindness. That will was her idea of a joke. Nasty old crone. I deserve her money.'

'Well,' said Mrs Penzler, in the clipped tones she normally reserved for badly-behaved kids, 'I'm not sure we'd all agree with that. We'll see what the police have to say.'

I gave Mrs Penzler the permission letter and picked up my school bag. Katie Brewer looked like she'd just been slapped on the face with a wet fish. I mouthed 'Sorry' to her. She shrugged and gave me a lop-sided smile as if to say, 'T'ch, parents, eh?'.

On the way out of school, Muddy caught me up. He'd been fixing one of the computers in the IT suite.

'That leak in your shed,' he said. 'Good news.'

'Great!' I said. 'I could do with some good news.'

'I've had a last minute cancellation,' said Muddy.

'Brilliant!'

'If I move some jobs around, I can treat your leak as a red alert emergency repair situation.'

'Excellent!'

'So I can get to it much sooner than I originally thought.'

'Fantastic! When?'

'Two weeks next Thursday.'

I grumbled to myself all the way home.

Case closed.

www.saxbysmart.co.uk

Log on for details of
an exciting competition!

Plus:
Saxby newsletter
Ask the Author
Book Disguisers
Writing Tips
and much more!